Adopting The Total Mentality Of Truthfulness

Anubhav Shrivastava

ISBN 978-93-5667-491-2
© Anubhav Shrivastava 2023
Published in India 2023 by Pencil

A brand of

One Point Six Technologies Pvt. Ltd.
123, Building J2, Shram Seva Premises,
Wadala Truck Terminal, Wadala (E)
Mumbai 400037, Maharashtra, INDIA
E connect@thepencilapp.com
W www.thepencilapp.com

DISCLAIMER: *The opinions expressed in this book are those of the authors and do not purport to reflect the views of the Publisher.*

Author biography

Hello, I'm Anubhav Shrivastava You Know Also (Anubhavauthor) ! - And I'm A Self Help Author & Life Coach.

Actually it was 2 years ago. My best friend whose name is Kartik. He asked me Going for a walk somewhere. Means somewhere on such a trip. But I didn't have money at that time. And some time ago my situation was like this. Spending the whole day with your friends, partying all the time. And was leading a very useless life. Sometimes too much anxiety and sometimes stress. All these things were in life. But then I and kartik remembered. That we had another friend whose name was sam. He used to party a lot like us earlier. But just recently 2,3 weeks ago. He had come to visit dubai. So I told kartik. Man, he is a friend of our company, who is studying with us from college. From where did so much money suddenly come on him? Kartik told me that he had met sam a few days back. sam told him that he is a digital marketer. And from that he has earned more than $ 10,000 in the last 7 months. I got choked after listening to kartik. Kartik told me that he keeps on learning things online, he is also a book reader. I didn't know the meaning of these things. I was shocked.

From that day onwards this curiosity got fixed in me. How did he earn so many $? I learned a lot from that time. I made many mentors from different fields. Learned many different things from him. I also started my own online startup which was related to watches. But alas he did not go. But I learned many things from the experience of that time. And then my earning was started through so much learning. And all my old bad habits were also gone.

Then I thought I should not keep these learnings and experiences confined to myself. It would be wise to share them with others.

Then I chose Books which was a better way. To reach out to those people and new learnings that enable them to truly see their life as a clarity. That's why I decided that I will tell you the life experience learning of others, and my own learning through the books written by me. I myself will go and meet people and write their life experience in the exact same book as they said.

And then I decided to become an author, a valuable author. Whose deep valuable life experiences learnings reached you.

♥ Anubhavauthor ~

CONTENTS

Introduction

My name is Anubhavauthor, and I've always been a firm believer in the power of mentors. Throughout my struggles and my journey towards adopting a total mentality of truthfulness, I have been fortunate enough to have met many different mentors who have shared their wisdom and insights with me. Each of these mentors has played a pivotal role in shaping my thinking and guiding me towards a deeper understanding of the value of truthfulness.

One of my earliest mentors was a successful entrepreneur named Raj. Raj was someone who had built a thriving business from scratch, and he was always willing to share his knowledge and experience with others. I met him at a networking event, and we hit it off immediately. Over time, he shared with me his insights on entrepreneurship, leadership, and the importance of being honest and transparent with one's employees and customers. His mentorship was invaluable, and I credit much of my success to his guidance.

Another mentor of mine was a spiritual teacher named Kavita. Kavita was someone who had devoted her life to helping others find inner peace and balance. She taught me the importance of being honest with oneself and of living with integrity. Her teachings helped me to see that truthfulness is not just about being honest with others, but about being true to oneself as well.

As I continued on my journey towards adopting a total mentality of truthfulness, I met many other mentors along the way. Each of them had their own unique insights and perspectives, and each played a role in shaping my thinking and guiding me towards a deeper understanding of the value of truthfulness.

It was during this time that I met my friend Sam. Sam was someone who had always believed in me, and he was one of my biggest supporters on my journey towards adopting a total mentality of truthfulness. One day, over coffee, he said something that would change my life forever.

"Anubhavauthor," he said, "you've learned so much from your mentors. You have a wealth of knowledge and experience that you can share with others. Have you ever thought about writing a book?"

At first, I was hesitant. I had never considered myself a writer, and the idea of putting my thoughts and ideas into a book was daunting. But the more I thought about it, the more I realized that Sam was right. I had learned so much from my mentors, and I had a unique perspective on the value of truthfulness that I wanted to share with others.

So, I set out to write a book. I spent months compiling my thoughts and ideas, and I drew upon the wisdom of my many mentors to craft a message that I felt could inspire and empower others. The result was a book titled "Adopting The Total Mentality Of Truthfulness."

As I reflect on my journey towards adopting a total mentality of truthfulness, I am struck by the importance of mentors. Each of the mentors I met along the way played a unique role in guiding me towards a deeper understanding of the value of truthfulness. Without their guidance and support, I may never have fully embraced the power of truthfulness in my life.

So, to anyone who is struggling on their own journey towards adopting a total mentality of truthfulness, I would encourage you to seek out mentors. Whether they are business leaders, spiritual teachers, or simply friends who believe in you, mentors can offer guidance and support that can make all the difference in your journey. And who knows, perhaps one day, you too will be inspired to share your own wisdom and insights with the world.

The process of writing the book was a challenging but rewarding one. As I delved deeper into the topic of truthfulness, I realized that there was so much more to explore and discover. I drew upon my own experiences, as well as those of my mentors, to craft a message that I hoped would resonate with readers.

As I wrote, I found that my own understanding of the power of truthfulness continued to evolve. I began to see how truthfulness not only shapes our personal and professional lives, but also has a profound impact on the world around us. When we are truthful with ourselves and others, we create a culture of honesty and integrity that can inspire positive change.

Through the process of writing the book, I also discovered a newfound passion for writing. I realized that I enjoyed sharing my thoughts and ideas with others, and that I wanted to continue doing so in the future. I began to explore other avenues for sharing my message, including public speaking and online content creation.

Looking back on my journey, I am grateful for the role that mentors have played in my life. They have not only guided me towards a deeper understanding of the value of truthfulness, but have also inspired me to share my own insights with others. I hope that my book will serve as a source of inspiration and empowerment for anyone who is on their own journey towards adopting a total mentality of truthfulness.

the power of mentors cannot be overstated. Whether you are embarking on a new career path, exploring a new hobby, or simply seeking personal growth, mentors can offer guidance and support that can help you to achieve your goals. And who knows, perhaps one day, you too will be inspired to share your own wisdom and insights with the world.

Quote

" When you see things as they are. So you can see the Truth"…

INTRODUCTION

CHAPTER ONE

Introduction

"The Power of Honesty: How Truthfulness Shapes Our Personal and Professional Lives"

The power of honesty cannot be overstated, as it shapes not only our personal lives, but also our professional lives. At the personal level, honesty is fundamental to building and maintaining trust in our relationships with others. When we are truthful with those around us, we establish a sense of integrity and reliability that fosters deeper connections and stronger bonds. Conversely, when we are dishonest or deceptive, we erode trust and create distance between ourselves and those we care about.

In romantic relationships, honesty is particularly important. It is often said that trust is the foundation of a healthy relationship, and trust cannot exist without honesty. When we are truthful with our partners about our thoughts, feelings, and actions, we open the door for true intimacy and connection. We demonstrate that we are willing to be vulnerable, which invites our partners to reciprocate and share their own vulnerabilities with us. On the other hand, when we lie or withhold the truth, we build walls and barriers that can ultimately lead to the breakdown of the relationship.

Honesty also plays a crucial role in our professional lives. At work, we interact with a diverse group of people, each with their own set of expectations and priorities. When we are honest with our colleagues and clients, we demonstrate that we are dependable and trustworthy. This builds a foundation of respect and credibility that can open doors to new opportunities and collaborations. It also enables us to communicate more effectively, as we can speak our minds without fear of reprisal or misunderstanding.

However, honesty in the workplace is not always easy. There are times when we may be tempted to stretch the truth or withhold information in order to avoid conflict or protect our interests. In these situations, it is important to remember that honesty is not just a moral imperative, but also a strategic one. When we are honest with our colleagues and clients, we build a reputation for integrity that can help us navigate challenging situations with greater ease. Conversely, when we are known for dishonesty, our credibility is undermined, and we may find ourselves shut out of important conversations and opportunities.

It is also important to recognize that honesty is not always black and white. There are times when we may need to balance our need for honesty with other ethical considerations, such as confidentiality or privacy. In these situations, it is important to weigh the pros and cons of various courses of action and make the decision that is most likely to preserve our integrity and build trust.

Ultimately, the power of honesty lies in its ability to shape not just our personal and professional lives, but also the world around us. When we are honest with ourselves and others, we create a culture of transparency and accountability that promotes fairness and equity. We become role models for others to emulate, and we inspire those around us to be truthful and authentic in their own lives. As such, honesty is not just a virtue, but a path to personal and collective growth and transformation.

However, it is important to acknowledge that honesty can also be difficult and even uncomfortable at times. It requires us to confront our own biases and assumptions, as well as those of others. It may require us to admit to our own mistakes or shortcomings, or to challenge the beliefs of those around us. But it is precisely this discomfort that makes honesty so powerful. When we are honest with ourselves and others, we create space for growth and learning, both individually and collectively.

the power of honesty cannot be overstated. It is a foundational value that shapes our personal and professional lives, and that has the potential to transform the world around us. By prioritizing honesty in our interactions with others, we build trust, credibility, and respect. We create a culture of transparency and accountability that promotes fairness and equity. And we become role models for others to follow, inspiring them to be truthful and authentic in their own lives. So let us strive to be honest in all that we do, and let us recognize the transformative power of this fundamental value.

The Science of Honesty: How Being Truthful Affects Our Mental and Emotional Health

Honesty is a fundamental aspect of our personal and professional lives. It's a trait that we all strive for, and one that we hope others possess as well. But did you know that honesty can also have a profound impact on our mental and emotional health?

Research has shown that being truthful is not only beneficial for our relationships, but also for our overall well-being. When we are truthful, we experience less stress and anxiety, and are more likely to feel a sense of purpose and fulfillment in our lives.

One reason for this is that when we are dishonest, we experience what's known as "cognitive dissonance." This is the discomfort that arises when our thoughts, beliefs, and actions are in conflict with one another. The more we lie or hide the truth, the greater this conflict becomes, leading to increased stress and anxiety.

On the other hand, when we are truthful, we experience a sense of freedom and release. We no longer have to worry about keeping up a façade or remembering our lies. This sense of relief can be incredibly empowering, leading to a greater sense of self-confidence and self-worth.

In addition to the mental benefits of honesty, research has also shown that being truthful can have a positive impact on our physical health. Studies have found that individuals who are honest tend to have lower levels of cortisol, a stress hormone that can lead to a host of health issues, including weight gain, cardiovascular disease, and impaired immune function.

But perhaps the most important benefit of honesty is the impact it can have on our relationships. When we are truthful with those around us, we build trust and respect, which are the foundation of any healthy relationship. By being open and honest with others, we create an environment where communication can thrive, and conflicts can be resolved in a healthy and constructive manner.

Of course, being truthful is not always easy. There are times when we may be tempted to hide the truth, or to sugarcoat things in order to avoid conflict. But the science is clear – being honest is essential for our mental and emotional health, and for our relationships with those around us.

So if you're struggling with being truthful, take heart – it's a skill that can be developed with practice. Start small by being honest with yourself, and then gradually work your way up to being honest with those around you. With time and effort, you'll find that honesty becomes a natural and empowering part of your life.

It's important to note, however, that honesty should always be balanced with kindness and compassion. While it's important to be truthful, it's equally important to consider the impact of our words and actions on those around us. Sometimes, being honest may mean having difficult conversations or making tough decisions, but it's important to approach these situations with empathy and understanding.

Another aspect of the science of honesty is the importance of self-reflection. By taking the time to reflect on our thoughts, feelings, and actions, we can gain a better understanding of ourselves and our values. This, in turn, can help us to be more honest with ourselves and others, as we learn to recognize and address areas where we may be out of alignment.

Ultimately, the science of honesty shows us that being truthful is not just a moral obligation, but a fundamental aspect of our well-being. By being honest with ourselves and those around us, we can build stronger, more meaningful relationships, experience less stress and anxiety, and live a more fulfilling and purposeful life.

So if you're looking to improve your mental and emotional health, start by embracing the power of honesty. Be truthful with yourself and those around you, and approach difficult situations with kindness and empathy. With time and practice, you'll find that honesty becomes a natural and empowering part of your life, and that the benefits of this powerful trait extend far beyond just the surface level of our interactions.

the science of honesty is a powerful reminder of the importance of truthfulness in shaping our mental and emotional health. By being truthful with ourselves and those around us, we can build stronger, more authentic relationships, experience less stress and anxiety, and live a more fulfilling and purposeful life.

It's important to remember that honesty is not always easy, and may require us to confront uncomfortable truths about ourselves or others. However, by approaching these situations with kindness and empathy, we can create a safe and supportive environment for growth and learning.

If you're looking to adopt a more honest and truthful mindset, start by taking small steps towards greater self-awareness and authenticity. Reflect on your values and motivations, and consider the impact of your words and actions on those around you. With time and practice, you'll find that honesty becomes a natural and empowering part of your life, and that the benefits of this powerful trait extend far beyond just the surface level of our interactions.

The Role of Honesty in Building Strong Personal Relationships and Friendships

Honesty is a fundamental aspect of building strong personal relationships and friendships. Without honesty, trust cannot exist, and without trust, a relationship cannot thrive. When we are honest with ourselves and those around us, we create a foundation of trust and mutual respect, which allows us to build deep and meaningful connections with others.

For example, let's take the story of two childhood friends, Maya and Olivia. Maya and Olivia had been friends since they were young, and over the years, their friendship had grown stronger and more meaningful. However, as they entered their teenage years, they began to grow apart, and their communication became strained and distant.

One day, Maya realized that she had been holding onto a secret that was weighing heavily on her heart. She had been struggling with depression for months, but had been too afraid to tell anyone, even her closest friends. However, she knew that in order to maintain her friendship with Olivia, she needed to be honest and open about her struggles.

So, Maya took a deep breath and sat down with Olivia, telling her everything that had been weighing on her heart. At first, Olivia was taken aback and unsure of how to respond, but as Maya spoke, she could see the pain and vulnerability in her friend's eyes. In that moment, Olivia realized how much she valued their friendship, and how much she wanted to support Maya through her struggles.

From that moment on, Maya and Olivia's friendship grew even stronger. They were able to be honest and open with each other, and they knew that no matter what challenges they faced, they could count on each other for support and guidance.

This story highlights the importance of honesty in building strong personal relationships and friendships. When we are honest with ourselves and those around us, we create a safe and supportive environment for growth and learning. We build trust and mutual respect, which allows us to connect with others on a deep and meaningful level.

Of course, being honest is not always easy, and may require us to confront uncomfortable truths about ourselves or others. However, by approaching these situations with kindness and empathy, we can create a safe and supportive environment for growth and learning.

Ultimately, the role of honesty in building strong personal relationships and friendships is one of the most important lessons we can learn. By being truthful with ourselves and those around us, we create a foundation of trust and mutual respect, which allows us to build deep and meaningful connections with others. So if you're looking to build stronger relationships and friendships, start by embracing the power of honesty, and watch as your connections with others grow stronger and more meaningful over time.

In addition to building strong personal relationships and friendships, honesty also has a significant impact on our mental and emotional health. When we are truthful with ourselves and others, we are able to let go of the weight of secrets and lies, and release ourselves from the burden of emotional baggage.

This is because living in honesty allows us to be true to ourselves, and to align our actions with our values and beliefs. When we are living in alignment with our true selves, we are able to experience a greater sense of inner peace, contentment, and fulfillment. On the other hand, when we are living in dishonesty, we are constantly battling with the inner conflict between our actions and our values, which can lead to feelings of guilt, shame, and anxiety.

Moreover, honesty also allows us to cultivate healthy communication and conflict resolution skills, which are essential in maintaining strong and healthy relationships. By being honest with ourselves and others, we are able to communicate our needs and boundaries, and to address any issues or conflicts that may arise in a respectful and constructive manner.

the role of honesty in building strong personal relationships and friendships cannot be overstated. When we embrace honesty and live in alignment with our true selves, we create a foundation of trust, mutual respect, and open communication, which allows us to build deep and meaningful connections with others. Additionally, living in honesty can also have a positive impact on our mental and emotional health, allowing us to experience greater levels of inner peace, contentment, and fulfillment. So if you're looking to build stronger relationships and live a more fulfilling life, start by embracing the power of honesty, and watch as your life begins to transform in meaningful and powerful ways.

Remember, honesty is not always easy. It requires courage, vulnerability, and a willingness to face the truth, even when it may be uncomfortable or difficult to accept. But the rewards of living in honesty are immeasurable, and the impact it can have on our relationships and our mental and emotional health is profound.

So if you find yourself struggling with dishonesty, whether it be in your personal or professional life, know that it is never too late to make a change. Start by being truthful with yourself, and examine the areas in which you may be living in dishonesty. Then, make a commitment to yourself and to those around you to embrace honesty and to live in alignment with your true self.

And remember, building strong personal relationships and friendships takes time and effort, but the rewards are worth it. By embracing the power of honesty, you can create deep and meaningful connections with others that will enrich your life in countless ways. So don't be afraid to be honest, to be vulnerable, and to build relationships based on trust, mutual respect, and open communication. You never know how your honesty and authenticity may inspire others to do the same, and create a ripple effect of positivity and transformation in the world.

Honesty in the Workplace: How Truthfulness Enhances Productivity and Team Dynamics

 Honesty is essential in the workplace, and it has a powerful impact on both productivity and team dynamics. When employees feel free to be honest and express their opinions, it fosters an environment of open communication and trust. This, in turn, enhances collaboration and teamwork, leading to increased productivity and success.

One example of the power of honesty in the workplace comes from my own experience. I worked for a company where the CEO was notoriously dishonest and manipulative. His lack of honesty created a toxic work environment where employees were afraid to speak up and share their ideas. This resulted in a lack of collaboration, stagnation of growth, and high employee turnover.

On the other hand, I also worked for a company where honesty was valued and encouraged. The leadership team actively sought out feedback from employees, and everyone felt comfortable expressing their thoughts and ideas. This led to a positive and productive work environment where everyone felt valued and respected. The company experienced tremendous growth, and employee turnover was low.

In addition to productivity, honesty also plays a critical role in team dynamics. When team members are honest with each other, they build trust and respect. This, in turn, leads to better collaboration and communication, which is essential for achieving shared goals.

I once worked on a project with a team where one member was not being honest about their progress. This caused the entire team to fall behind and miss important deadlines. Once the dishonesty was addressed, the team was able to regroup, communicate more effectively, and work collaboratively to catch up and finish the project on time.

On the other hand, I also worked on a project where the team members were honest and transparent with each other. We were able to share our ideas, identify areas where we needed help, and work together to achieve our goals. This led to a successful project outcome and a sense of pride and accomplishment among the team.

honesty is a critical component of success in the workplace. When honesty is valued and encouraged, it leads to increased productivity, positive team dynamics, and success for both the company and its employees. By fostering a culture of honesty, companies can create an environment where employees feel valued and respected, and where collaboration and communication are at the forefront of success.

In order to cultivate honesty in the workplace, it is important for leaders to lead by example. Leaders must be honest and transparent with their team members, and actively seek out feedback from employees. They should create a safe space for employees to share their thoughts and ideas, and provide constructive feedback in return.

It is also important to establish clear communication channels and set expectations for honesty and transparency from the outset. This includes setting clear goals, deadlines, and milestones, and communicating progress updates regularly. When everyone is on the same page, it is easier to stay honest and hold each other accountable.

Finally, it is important to acknowledge and address any instances of dishonesty in the workplace. This means addressing any conflicts or misunderstandings as soon as they arise, and being willing to have difficult conversations when necessary. By addressing dishonesty head-on, it sends a clear message to employees that honesty is valued and important in the workplace.

the role of honesty in the workplace is critical to achieving success. When honesty is valued and encouraged, it creates a positive and productive work environment, and leads to increased productivity and success for both the company and its employees. By establishing a culture of honesty, transparency, and open communication, companies can build strong teams and achieve shared goals.

The Ethics of Truthfulness: Balancing Honesty with Privacy and Confidentiality

The ethics of truthfulness are a complex and nuanced subject, especially when it comes to balancing honesty with privacy and confidentiality. In both our personal and professional lives, there are situations where we are faced with difficult decisions about whether to be completely truthful or to withhold information to protect someone's privacy or confidentiality.

In the workplace, employees often have access to sensitive and confidential information, such as financial data, personal information, or trade secrets. In such situations, it is important for employees to balance the need for honesty with the need to protect privacy and confidentiality. For example, an employee may be asked by a supervisor to provide information about a colleague's performance, but may feel uncomfortable sharing this information due to concerns about confidentiality. In such cases, it is important to find a way to balance the need for honesty with the need to respect confidentiality, perhaps by providing general feedback without divulging specific information.

Similarly, in our personal lives, we may be faced with situations where we need to balance honesty with privacy. For example, if a close friend confides in us about a personal struggle, we may need to consider whether it is appropriate to share this information with others. In such cases, it is important to respect our friend's privacy, while also being honest and true to our own values.

Finding the right balance between honesty and privacy requires careful consideration and thoughtful decision-making. It is important to consider the potential consequences of our actions, and to be mindful of the impact they may have on others. It is also important to be willing to have difficult conversations and to seek out guidance and advice when necessary.

the ethics of truthfulness require us to balance the need for honesty with the need to respect privacy and confidentiality. While there may be times when it is difficult to find the right balance, it is important to approach these situations with care and thoughtfulness. By doing so, we can build trust and respect in our personal and professional relationships, and ensure that we are acting with integrity and respect for others.

Ultimately, the ethics of truthfulness are about balancing our obligations to tell the truth with our responsibilities to respect the privacy and confidentiality of others. This requires us to consider the impact of our actions on others, and to weigh the potential benefits of being honest against the potential harms of violating someone's privacy or confidentiality.

At the same time, we must also be honest with ourselves, and with our own values and principles. It is important to reflect on our own motives and intentions, and to be willing to take responsibility for our actions and decisions.

In today's world, where information is shared and disseminated at an unprecedented rate, the ethics of truthfulness have never been more important. As individuals and as a society, we must find ways to navigate this complex landscape with integrity and respect for others. By doing so, we can build strong relationships, foster trust and transparency, and create a more just and equitable world for all.

Cultivating a Culture of Honesty: How Leaders Can Foster Truthfulness in Their Organizations

Honesty is an essential value for any successful organization, but creating a culture of honesty is no easy feat. Leaders must be deliberate in their efforts to foster truthfulness, and must model the behavior they wish to see in their employees. By creating an environment that values honesty and transparency, leaders can cultivate a culture of trust that empowers employees to speak up, collaborate more effectively, and work towards shared goals.

One of the most important steps leaders can take is to communicate the importance of honesty clearly and consistently. This means setting clear expectations for employees, and demonstrating a commitment to transparency and accountability. Leaders should encourage their team to speak up when they see something that isn't right, and to share their ideas and concerns openly and honestly. This can help to create an atmosphere of mutual respect and trust, and can lead to better collaboration and problem-solving.

Another key aspect of cultivating a culture of honesty is building trust with employees. Leaders must be willing to listen to their team, and to act on their feedback and suggestions. They must also be willing to admit when they are wrong, and to take responsibility for their actions. By doing so, they can model the behavior they wish to see in their employees, and create an atmosphere of openness and accountability.

Finally, leaders must be willing to take proactive steps to prevent dishonesty and unethical behavior. This means developing and enforcing clear policies and procedures that encourage ethical behavior, and holding employees accountable when they violate these standards. By doing so, leaders can create a culture of honesty that fosters trust, collaboration, and accountability.

Cultivating a culture of honesty is an ongoing process that requires ongoing effort and attention. It requires leaders to be honest and transparent themselves, to build trust with their employees, and to take proactive steps to prevent dishonesty and unethical behavior. By doing so, they can create a workplace culture that empowers employees to be their best selves, and to work towards shared goals with honesty and integrity.

honesty is an essential value that should be prioritized in any organization. Leaders must understand that cultivating a culture of honesty is a process that requires deliberate effort and attention, and must be willing to model the behavior they wish to see in their employees. By communicating the importance of honesty, building trust with their team, and taking proactive steps to prevent dishonesty and unethical behavior, leaders can create a workplace culture that values openness, transparency, and accountability. This can lead to better collaboration, improved productivity, and a more fulfilling work environment for everyone. Ultimately, the success of any organization depends on its ability to foster a culture of honesty, and leaders must take this responsibility seriously if they wish to achieve their goals and inspire their team to do the same.

Overview of the book's key concepts and themes

 Adopting the Total Mentality of Truthfulness is a powerful guide to living a life of honesty and authenticity. The book is written by Anubhavauthor, who draws on his personal experiences to explore the many benefits of being truthful in all aspects of life. The book covers a wide range of topics related to honesty and truthfulness, including how it can enhance personal relationships, boost productivity in the workplace, and even improve mental and emotional health.

One of the key concepts explored in the book is the importance of self-awareness. Anubhavauthor argues that self-awareness is a vital component of being truthful, as it allows us to understand our own motivations and desires, and to be honest with ourselves about our strengths and weaknesses. By being honest with ourselves, we can develop greater clarity about our goals and values, and make better decisions that are in alignment with who we truly are.

Another key theme in the book is the relationship between honesty and trust. Anubhavauthor stresses the importance of building trust in all aspects of life, whether it is in personal relationships, the workplace, or in society at large. He argues that honesty is the foundation of trust, and that being truthful and transparent with others is the best way to establish strong, lasting relationships built on mutual respect and understanding.

The book also explores the ethics of honesty, and the challenges that can arise when balancing truthfulness with privacy and confidentiality. Anubhavauthor acknowledges that there are times when it may be necessary to keep certain information private, and that this can sometimes conflict with the value of honesty. He provides guidance on how to navigate these complex situations, and emphasizes the importance of always striving to act with integrity and in a way that is consistent with our values.

Throughout the book, Anubhavauthor shares many personal stories and anecdotes to illustrate his points and make the concepts come alive. He writes in a clear and engaging style, and his passion for the topic shines through on every page. The book is both informative and inspiring, and provides readers with a wealth of practical advice and actionable steps to help them live a more truthful and authentic life.

Adopting the Total Mentality of Truthfulness is a powerful guide to living a life of honesty and authenticity. It covers a wide range of topics related to honesty and truthfulness, and provides readers with a wealth of practical advice and actionable steps to help them cultivate greater self-awareness, build stronger relationships, and achieve greater success in all areas of life.

The Psychology Of Honesty

CHAPTER TWO

The Psychology Of Honesty

The concept of honesty is an integral aspect of our daily lives, influencing the way we perceive ourselves, interact with others, and navigate the world around us. From personal identity to relationships, communication, and leadership, the role of honesty is multidimensional and multifaceted, shaping the psychological landscape of our lives in powerful ways.

The psychology of honesty is a field of study that seeks to understand the cognitive and emotional processes that underlie our capacity for truthfulness and integrity. Through research, experimentation, and observation, psychologists have shed light on the complex interplay between honesty and various aspects of our lives, offering insights into how we can cultivate a greater sense of authenticity, trust, and connection in our interactions with others.

At the heart of the psychology of honesty is the understanding that truth-telling is not simply a matter of ethics or morality, but rather a fundamental aspect of human psychology. Our ability to be honest is shaped by a range of psychological factors, including our self-perception, cognitive biases, social context, and emotional state.

As we navigate the complex terrain of relationships, communication, and self-perception, the role of honesty takes on added significance, influencing the way we see ourselves, how we are perceived by others, and the quality of our interactions. Through the lens of the psychology of honesty, we can begin to understand the ways in which our relationship with truthfulness shapes our lives, and how we can harness its power to cultivate greater well-being and fulfillment.

This book explores the dynamic landscape of the psychology of honesty, offering a comprehensive examination of the factors that influence our capacity for truthfulness and integrity. From personal identity to relationships, communication, and leadership, each chapter explores a different facet of the role of honesty in our lives, drawing on the latest research and real-world examples to offer insights and practical strategies for cultivating greater authenticity, trust, and connection.

Whether you are seeking to improve your relationships, communication skills, or leadership abilities, the insights and strategies offered in this book will provide you with the tools and knowledge to harness the power of honesty and integrity in your life. From building stronger personal connections to leading with authenticity and compassion, the psychology of honesty offers a pathway to greater fulfillment, success, and well-being, both personally and professionally.

The role of honesty in personal identity and self-esteem

Honesty is a fundamental aspect of human behavior that shapes personal identity and self-esteem. When we are honest with ourselves and others, we build trust and respect in our relationships, both with ourselves and others. This trust and respect are essential to building a strong and healthy sense of personal identity and self-esteem.

Consider the story of Jane, a young woman who struggled with honesty throughout her teenage years. She found it difficult to be honest with herself and others about her true feelings and desires, often going along with what others wanted or expected of her. This led to a lack of trust and respect in her relationships, both with herself and others, and ultimately damaged her sense of personal identity and self-esteem.

However, Jane eventually realized the importance of honesty in building a strong sense of self. She began to practice being honest with herself and others, even if it was uncomfortable or difficult. This honesty allowed her to establish trust and respect in her relationships, leading to a healthier sense of personal identity and self-esteem.

Another example is John, who had struggled with low self-esteem for years due to a lack of honesty in his personal life. He would often lie to himself and others about his accomplishments and abilities, leading to a false sense of self-worth that left him feeling empty and unfulfilled.

But when John started to be honest about his true abilities and accomplishments, he found that he was able to build a more genuine sense of self-esteem. His newfound honesty helped him to build stronger relationships with others, which in turn helped him to develop a greater sense of personal identity and purpose.

These stories illustrate the importance of honesty in building personal identity and self-esteem. When we are honest with ourselves and others, we build a foundation of trust and respect that can help us to develop a strong and healthy sense of self. This sense of self is crucial to our overall well-being and happiness, as it provides us with a clear understanding of our values and purpose in life.

In addition to building personal identity and self-esteem, honesty can also help us to become more resilient in the face of adversity. When we are honest with ourselves and others about our strengths and weaknesses, we are better able to face challenges and setbacks with a sense of confidence and self-assurance. This allows us to bounce back from difficult situations and continue to move forward with a positive outlook on life.

Overall, the role of honesty in personal identity and self-esteem cannot be overstated. By practicing honesty in our daily lives, we can build trust and respect in our relationships and develop a stronger sense of self. This can lead to greater happiness, resilience, and overall well-being, making honesty a valuable tool for personal growth and development.

honesty plays a critical role in personal identity and self-esteem. When we are honest with ourselves and others, we build trust and establish a sense of integrity that can boost our self-esteem and self-worth. On the other hand, when we are dishonest, we may experience feelings of guilt, shame, and anxiety, which can damage our sense of self and identity. Being honest with ourselves and others requires us to be vulnerable and open to the possibility of rejection or disapproval, but it is ultimately worth it for the sense of peace and self-assurance that comes with living authentically. By embracing honesty as a core value in our lives, we can build a strong sense of self and self-esteem that can help us navigate life's challenges with greater confidence and resilience.

The Relationship between Honesty and Mental Health: A Psychological Perspective

Honesty is a crucial aspect of mental health and well-being. As human beings, we are wired to seek out authenticity and truthfulness in our relationships and interactions with others. But the relationship between honesty and mental health goes beyond our social connections. It also plays a key role in shaping our internal psychological landscape and our overall sense of well-being.

At its core, honesty is about being true to ourselves and our values. When we live in alignment with our beliefs and principles, we experience a sense of authenticity and integrity that can have a profound impact on our mental health. In contrast, when we live in a state of dishonesty, we create a dissonance between our internal world and our external actions, which can lead to feelings of guilt, shame, and anxiety.

One of the key ways that honesty impacts our mental health is by fostering a sense of self-awareness and self-acceptance. When we are honest with ourselves about our thoughts, feelings, and behaviors, we are better able to identify areas where we need to grow and change. This level of self-awareness can lead to increased self-esteem, self-confidence, and a greater sense of control over our lives.

In addition to promoting self-awareness, honesty is also essential for healthy relationships. When we are truthful with our loved ones, we build a foundation of trust and open communication that can help us weather the ups and downs of life. On the other hand, when we are dishonest with our partners or friends, we create a rift in the relationship that can be difficult to repair.

Research has also shown that honesty can play a role in our physical health. Studies have found that people who engage in dishonest behavior, such as lying or cheating, are more likely to experience stress and negative health outcomes, including cardiovascular disease and chronic pain.

Overall, the relationship between honesty and mental health is complex and multifaceted. But one thing is clear: being honest with ourselves and others is essential for living a healthy, fulfilling life. By embracing honesty, we can cultivate a sense of self-awareness, build strong relationships, and promote overall well-being.

the relationship between honesty and mental health is complex and multifaceted. Honesty is an essential aspect of maintaining good mental health, as it allows individuals to confront and work through their emotions and experiences, leading to greater self-awareness and acceptance. At the same time, it is important to balance honesty with sensitivity, as being too honest or harsh can cause unnecessary harm to oneself or others. Honesty is also critical in therapeutic settings, where it is necessary to establish a safe and trusting relationship between therapist and client. By being honest with oneself and others, individuals can cultivate better mental health, stronger relationships, and a greater sense of self-worth and purpose. It is clear that honesty is an integral part of our psychological well-being and can greatly impact our overall quality of life.

The Art of Self-Honesty: How to Overcome Self-Deception and Live a Fulfilling Life

Self-deception is a common human tendency that can lead to a lot of problems in life. Many people engage in self-deception because they find it difficult to confront their own flaws or to admit when they are wrong. However, self-honesty is an essential aspect of personal growth and well-being. In this article, we will explore the art of self-honesty and how it can help you live a fulfilling life.

The first step to cultivating self-honesty is to recognize when you are engaging in self-deception. This requires a great deal of self-awareness and a willingness to be honest with yourself. For example, if you find yourself making excuses for your behavior or blaming others for your problems, it may be a sign that you are not being completely honest with yourself.

Once you have recognized your self-deception, the next step is to start examining your beliefs and assumptions. Many people hold onto beliefs that are not based in reality or that are no longer relevant to their lives. By examining your beliefs and assumptions, you can identify those that are holding you back and start to let them go.

Another important aspect of self-honesty is the ability to accept feedback from others. When someone points out a flaw or mistake, it can be tempting to become defensive or to dismiss the feedback as unimportant. However, by being open to feedback and willing to learn from others, you can gain a better understanding of your own strengths and weaknesses.

Self-honesty can also help you to set realistic goals and make better decisions. By being honest with yourself about your abilities and limitations, you can avoid setting yourself up for failure or making poor choices. Instead, you can focus on developing your strengths and finding ways to work around your limitations.

In addition to these benefits, self-honesty can also lead to greater self-esteem and confidence. When you are honest with yourself about your flaws and limitations, you can approach challenges with a sense of humility and openness. This can help you to develop a stronger sense of self-worth and to feel more confident in your ability to overcome obstacles.

Overall, the art of self-honesty is an essential aspect of personal growth and well-being. By being honest with yourself, you can overcome self-deception, set realistic goals, and make better decisions. This can lead to greater self-esteem and confidence, as well as a greater sense of fulfillment in life. So, take the time to examine your beliefs and assumptions, accept feedback from others, and cultivate a sense of self-awareness and honesty. Your future self will thank you for it.

self-honesty is a vital tool for personal growth and fulfillment. It enables us to confront and overcome our flaws and shortcomings, and to live in alignment with our values and goals. The process of cultivating self-honesty requires self-reflection, self-awareness, and a willingness to embrace discomfort and vulnerability. It can be challenging, but the rewards are well worth the effort. By acknowledging and accepting our truths, we can develop a stronger sense of self, deepen our relationships with others, and live a more authentic and meaningful life.

The Ethics of Honesty in Professional Psychology: Balancing Confidentiality and Truth-Telling

The ethics of honesty is a crucial aspect of professional psychology. The role of psychologists is to help individuals manage their emotional and psychological issues, while also adhering to the ethical principles of their profession. Honesty is an important part of this process. However, there are situations where the need to maintain confidentiality conflicts with the need to be honest with clients.

Psychologists are expected to maintain a high level of confidentiality in their work with clients. This means that they cannot disclose any personal information about their clients to anyone, without the client's express permission. However, there are situations where the need to maintain confidentiality can be in conflict with the need to be honest. For example, if a client is at risk of harming themselves or others, the psychologist has a duty to warn the potential victims, even if it means breaking the client's confidentiality.

Psychologists must also be honest in their assessments of their clients. If a psychologist believes that a client is not suitable for a particular treatment, they must be honest about it, even if it means losing the client. Similarly, if a psychologist believes that a client is not making progress, they must be honest and suggest alternative approaches to treatment.

The issue of honesty is also relevant when it comes to research. Psychologists must be honest in reporting their findings, even if they do not support their hypotheses or theories. This means that they cannot manipulate their data or results to fit a predetermined outcome.

One of the ways that psychologists can maintain honesty in their profession is by being transparent with their clients. This means being upfront about the nature of their work, the limits of confidentiality, and the potential risks and benefits of treatment. This can help to build trust between the psychologist and the client, which is crucial for successful outcomes.

It is also important for psychologists to acknowledge their own biases and limitations. This means recognizing when their own beliefs, values, or experiences might be influencing their work with clients. It also means being open to feedback from clients, and being willing to adjust their approach if it is not working.

the ethics of honesty in professional psychology are complex and multifaceted. Psychologists must balance the need to maintain confidentiality with the need to be honest with their clients. They must also be honest in their assessments and research, and transparent in their work with clients. By being honest and transparent, psychologists can build trust with their clients, and help them to manage their psychological and emotional issues in a healthy and effective way.

honesty is a crucial component of our personal, professional, and social lives. It helps us to build strong relationships, maintain trust, and achieve mental well-being. Honesty, however, is not always easy, and it requires a great deal of courage, vulnerability, and self-reflection. The journey towards becoming a more honest person may be challenging, but it is also rewarding. It can lead to a sense of inner peace, personal growth, and a more fulfilling life.

The importance of honesty is particularly salient in the field of psychology, where it is essential for maintaining the trust and confidence of clients. However, psychologists must also navigate the complex ethical considerations surrounding confidentiality and truth-telling. They must find a balance between respecting the privacy of their clients and being truthful in their assessments and treatments. This requires careful consideration, ethical decision-making, and a commitment to the well-being of their clients.

the psychology of honesty is a vast and complex topic, with implications for every aspect of our lives. It is an ongoing journey, one that requires self-reflection, vulnerability, and a commitment to personal growth. By cultivating a culture of honesty, we can build stronger relationships, achieve mental well-being, and live more fulfilling lives.

Honesty in the Digital Age: The Psychological Impacts of Deception and Trust in Online Communication

Honesty is a fundamental value in human relationships, whether they take place in person or online. However, the rise of digital communication has brought new challenges to the way people interact, and the internet has created an environment in which it is easy to deceive or mislead others. As a result, honesty and trust have become more important than ever before, and their absence can have significant psychological impacts on individuals and their relationships.

The anonymity and perceived distance provided by the internet can make it easier for people to deceive others, whether intentionally or not. This is particularly true in contexts where people feel less accountable for their actions, such as social media, online dating, or anonymous message boards. People can easily hide behind fake names or profiles, or use tactics such as catfishing to misrepresent themselves to others. These actions can lead to a lack of trust, and can erode the psychological well-being of those who have been deceived.

The psychological impacts of deception and the absence of trust in online communication can be significant. In many cases, people who have been deceived or misled online may experience feelings of betrayal, anger, and disappointment. These emotions can lead to a decrease in self-esteem and confidence, as well as a sense of confusion and uncertainty about one's own judgment. Additionally, individuals may feel a sense of isolation, as they struggle to come to terms with the fact that they have been deceived by someone they believed they could trust.

Furthermore, the absence of honesty and trust in online communication can also have an impact on the larger social fabric. When people do not trust each other, it can lead to a breakdown in social cohesion and cooperation. This can be particularly problematic in contexts where trust is essential, such as online marketplaces, social movements, or political discourse. Without trust, people may be less likely to engage with others, share information, or work together towards common goals.

Despite these challenges, there are ways in which people can promote honesty and trust in online communication. For example, individuals can take steps to verify the identity of those they communicate with online, or use services such as background checks or online reputation management tools to help them make more informed decisions about who to trust. Additionally, people can be more mindful of their own behavior, and strive to be honest and transparent in their online interactions.

Ultimately, the digital age has created new challenges for honesty and trust in human relationships. However, it is important to remember that these challenges are not insurmountable, and that there are ways in which people can work to build more honest and trustworthy online communities. By taking steps to verify the identity of others and being mindful of our own behavior, we can create a more positive and supportive online environment, one that promotes honesty, trust, and respect.

Moreover, it is important to recognize that honesty and trust are values that are crucial for healthy and fulfilling relationships, both online and offline. By prioritizing these values, we can build stronger connections with others, and create a sense of safety and security in our online interactions. When we are honest and transparent with others, we give them the opportunity to trust us, and we can create a more open and supportive community.

honesty and trust are essential for healthy and fulfilling human relationships, and their absence in online communication can have significant psychological impacts. The rise of digital communication has made it easier for people to deceive others, but it has also provided new opportunities for building trust and fostering honesty. By being mindful of our own behavior and taking steps to verify the identity of others, we can create a more positive and supportive online environment, one that promotes honesty, trust, and respect. It is up to each individual to take responsibility for their own actions and to work towards building a more honest and trustworthy online community.

Honesty and Self-Reflection: Building a Strong Personal Identity

Honesty and self-reflection are two essential components in building a strong personal identity. When individuals are honest with themselves about their strengths and weaknesses, they can develop a clearer understanding of their own identity, which in turn leads to increased confidence, self-esteem, and a sense of purpose.

Self-reflection is the process of examining one's thoughts, feelings, and experiences, and gaining a deeper understanding of oneself. Through this process, individuals can identify their core values, beliefs, and goals, as well as their areas of strength and weakness. This can be a difficult process, as it requires individuals to be honest with themselves about their flaws and shortcomings, but it is an essential step in building a strong personal identity.

Honesty is a crucial component of self-reflection. It requires individuals to be truthful with themselves about their strengths and weaknesses, and to acknowledge areas where they may need to improve. Without honesty, self-reflection becomes ineffective, as individuals may be unwilling to confront the areas of their lives that require change.

When individuals engage in self-reflection and are honest with themselves, they can develop a stronger sense of personal identity. They can identify their unique qualities and characteristics, and can gain a better understanding of their own values and beliefs. This increased self-awareness can lead to greater self-esteem and confidence, as individuals feel more comfortable and secure in their own skin.

Furthermore, self-reflection and honesty can help individuals develop a sense of purpose and direction in life. By identifying their values and beliefs, individuals can develop a clearer sense of what they want to achieve in life and the goals they need to work towards. This can provide a sense of motivation and direction, as individuals work towards building a life that aligns with their values and beliefs.

However, being honest with oneself is not always easy. It requires individuals to confront their flaws and shortcomings, and to acknowledge areas where they may need to improve. This can be a difficult and uncomfortable process, but it is essential for personal growth and development.

In addition, being honest with oneself can also lead to greater authenticity in one's relationships with others. When individuals are honest about who they are, they are more likely to attract people who accept and appreciate them for who they are. This can lead to more meaningful and fulfilling relationships, as individuals feel comfortable being themselves and do not have to hide behind a façade.

honesty and self-reflection are two essential components in building a strong personal identity. Through self-reflection, individuals can identify their unique qualities, values, and beliefs, and gain a clearer sense of direction in life. Honesty is crucial in this process, as it requires individuals to be truthful with themselves about their flaws and shortcomings. While this process may be uncomfortable and difficult, it is essential for personal growth and development, and can lead to increased self-esteem, confidence, and a sense of purpose. Ultimately, by being honest with ourselves, we can build a strong and authentic personal identity that allows us to live our lives with greater intention and fulfillment.

Authenticity and Self-Esteem: How Honesty Impacts Our Self-Perception

Authenticity is the state of being true to oneself and one's values. It involves being honest with oneself and with others about who we truly are, including our strengths and weaknesses, values, beliefs, and desires. When individuals are authentic, they are able to express themselves in a genuine and sincere way, and this can have a positive impact on their self-esteem.

Self-esteem is a person's overall sense of self-worth and confidence in their abilities. It is shaped by a variety of factors, including past experiences, social interactions, and personal beliefs. Honesty and authenticity play an important role in shaping one's self-esteem, as they allow individuals to develop a more positive and realistic self-perception.

When individuals are honest and authentic with themselves, they are able to acknowledge their strengths and weaknesses, without judgment or criticism. This can lead to a more balanced and realistic self-perception, which in turn can have a positive impact on their self-esteem. By accepting and valuing themselves for who they are, individuals can develop a greater sense of self-worth, which can lead to increased confidence and a more positive outlook on life.

In contrast, when individuals are not authentic or honest with themselves, they may develop a distorted self-perception, which can have a negative impact on their self-esteem. For example, individuals who are constantly trying to present a certain image or facade may develop a sense of self that is based on external validation rather than their own values and beliefs. This can lead to a fragile self-esteem, as individuals may feel like they are constantly trying to live up to the expectations of others, rather than being true to themselves.

Moreover, when individuals are not authentic or honest with themselves, they may struggle with feelings of self-doubt and insecurity. They may feel like they are not good enough or that they do not measure up to the expectations of others. This can lead to a negative self-image, which can in turn impact their self-esteem.

On the other hand, when individuals are honest and authentic with themselves, they can develop a more positive and empowering self-perception. By accepting and valuing themselves for who they are, individuals can develop a stronger sense of self-worth, which can lead to increased confidence and a more positive outlook on life. This, in turn, can have a positive impact on their overall well-being and quality of life.

authenticity and honesty are essential in shaping our self-perception and self-esteem. When individuals are authentic and honest with themselves, they are able to develop a more positive and realistic self-perception, which can lead to increased self-worth and confidence. On the other hand, when individuals are not authentic or honest with themselves, they may develop a distorted self-perception, which can have a negative impact on their self-esteem. By being true to ourselves and our values, we can develop a more positive and empowering self-perception, which can have a positive impact on our overall well-being and quality of life.

The Cost of Deception: How Dishonesty Can Damage Self-Esteem and Identity

Deception is a behavior that is often used to gain advantage or protect oneself from negative consequences. However, while dishonesty may provide short-term benefits, the long-term costs of deception can be significant, including damage to one's self-esteem and personal identity.

One way that deception can damage self-esteem is by creating a sense of guilt or shame. When individuals engage in deceptive behavior, they often know that they are doing something wrong, and this can lead to feelings of guilt or shame. Over time, these feelings can erode self-esteem and make individuals feel unworthy or undeserving of respect and admiration.

Moreover, deception can also damage self-esteem by creating a sense of inauthenticity. When individuals engage in deceptive behavior, they are essentially presenting a false version of themselves to others. This can create a sense of disconnection between their true selves and the persona they present to the world. Over time, this disconnection can erode self-esteem and make individuals feel like they are living a lie.

Furthermore, deception can also damage personal identity by eroding a sense of integrity and authenticity. When individuals engage in deceptive behavior, they are essentially betraying their own values and beliefs. This can lead to a sense of self-betrayal and erode the sense of integrity that is fundamental to personal identity. Over time, this erosion of integrity can damage one's self-concept and make it difficult to know who they truly are.

The costs of deception can also impact relationships with others. When individuals engage in deceptive behavior, they are essentially violating the trust that others have placed in them. This can damage relationships and make it difficult for others to trust or respect them in the future. Over time, this erosion of trust can damage one's sense of self-worth and lead to a negative self-image.

Moreover, when individuals engage in deception, they may also experience fear and anxiety. They may worry about being caught, or fear the consequences of their actions. This can lead to a chronic sense of stress and anxiety, which can further damage self-esteem and personal identity.

the costs of deception can be significant, including damage to self-esteem, personal identity, and relationships with others. When individuals engage in deceptive behavior, they may experience guilt, shame, inauthenticity, erosion of integrity, fear, and anxiety. Over time, these negative consequences can erode one's sense of self-worth and make it difficult to know who they truly are. By being honest and authentic with oneself and others, individuals can avoid the damaging costs of deception and build a stronger sense of self-esteem and personal identity.

The Connection between Honesty and Self-Worth: A Psychological Perspective

The connection between honesty and self-worth is a complex and multi-faceted issue that has been the subject of much research and debate within the field of psychology. At the heart of this issue lies the question of how our sense of self-worth is shaped by our willingness to be honest with ourselves and others.

One of the key ways in which honesty is related to self-worth is through the concept of authenticity. Authenticity is the degree to which we are true to ourselves, and it is widely recognized as an important component of self-esteem and well-being. When we are honest with ourselves and others, we are more likely to be authentic, because we are not hiding anything or pretending to be someone we are not. This sense of authenticity can help to boost our self-esteem and make us feel more confident and secure in ourselves.

On the other hand, when we are not honest with ourselves or others, we can experience a range of negative emotions that can erode our sense of self-worth. For example, if we lie to someone or try to hide something, we may feel guilty or ashamed, and these feelings can lead to a sense of worthlessness or inadequacy. In addition, if we are not honest with ourselves about our own strengths and weaknesses, we may be more likely to engage in self-criticism and negative self-talk, which can also undermine our self-worth.

Another way in which honesty is related to self-worth is through the concept of trust. Trust is an important part of any healthy relationship, and it is built on a foundation of honesty and integrity. When we are honest with others, we are more likely to be trusted and respected, and this can help to boost our sense of self-worth. On the other hand, if we are not honest with others, we may find that we are not trusted or respected, and this can lead to feelings of rejection or disconnection.

Furthermore, honesty is essential in maintaining healthy relationships. When we are honest with ourselves and others, we are more likely to be able to communicate effectively and resolve conflicts in a productive manner. This can help to strengthen our relationships and deepen our sense of connection with others, which in turn can help to boost our self-worth.

However, being honest can also be difficult, especially in situations where the truth may be uncomfortable or painful. It can be tempting to lie or withhold information in order to avoid conflict or protect ourselves from negative consequences. But in the long run, these behaviors can actually do more harm than good, both to our relationships and to our sense of self-worth. Therefore, it is important to find ways to be honest in a compassionate and constructive way, while also taking care to respect the feelings and needs of others.

the connection between honesty and self-worth is a complex and multifaceted issue that touches on many aspects of our psychological and emotional well-being. Through being honest with ourselves and others, we can build a sense of authenticity, trust, and connection that can help to boost our self-esteem and sense of self-worth. However, being honest can also be challenging, and it is important to approach this issue with compassion and care, both for ourselves and for others. By doing so, we can build healthy, fulfilling relationships and lead happier, more fulfilling lives.

Cultivating a Culture of Honesty: The Role of Community and Support in Fostering Positive Self-Image

Cultivating a culture of honesty is a powerful way to foster positive self-image, and the role of community and support in this process cannot be overstated. When we live in a culture that values honesty and integrity, we are more likely to feel secure and confident in ourselves, because we know that we are living in a world that is grounded in truth and authenticity.

The first step in cultivating a culture of honesty is to create a safe and supportive community. When we feel supported by others, we are more likely to be open and honest with ourselves and with others. This support can take many forms, from close friendships and family relationships to professional communities and social networks. When we have people in our lives who we can trust and who we feel comfortable being ourselves around, we are more likely to be honest about our thoughts, feelings, and experiences.

Another important factor in fostering a culture of honesty is creating a sense of accountability. When we know that our actions and decisions will be scrutinized by others, we are more likely to act in a way that is consistent with our values and beliefs. This can be achieved through a variety of mechanisms, from social norms and expectations to more formal structures like laws and regulations. When we know that we are part of a community that holds us accountable, we are more likely to act in a way that is honest and authentic.

However, creating a culture of honesty also requires a degree of vulnerability. When we are honest with others, we are opening ourselves up to the possibility of judgment and criticism. This can be a scary prospect, and it is understandable that many people might be hesitant to be completely honest with others. But by taking this risk and being open and honest with others, we create an environment in which others feel comfortable being honest as well. This can lead to a virtuous cycle in which honesty and authenticity are reinforced and celebrated, creating a culture in which positive self-image and self-worth are nurtured.

Ultimately, creating a culture of honesty is about creating an environment in which people feel safe and supported in being themselves. When we live in a culture that values honesty and integrity, we are more likely to feel secure and confident in ourselves, because we know that we are living in a world that is grounded in truth and authenticity. By building supportive communities and creating a sense of accountability, we can foster this culture of honesty and create a space in which positive self-image and self-worth can flourish.

cultivating a culture of honesty is an essential component of fostering positive self-image and self-worth. By creating safe and supportive communities, fostering accountability, and embracing vulnerability, we can create an environment in which honesty and authenticity are valued and celebrated. This can lead to a virtuous cycle in which honesty and authenticity are reinforced and positive self-image and self-worth are nurtured. By embracing the role of community and support in this process, we can build a culture that values honesty and integrity, and creates a world in which we can all feel secure and confident in ourselves.

The benefits of honesty in relationships and communication

The benefits of honesty in relationships and communication are countless. Honesty is the foundation of any healthy and lasting relationship, whether it be romantic or platonic. When we are honest with ourselves and with others, we create a space of trust and understanding that allows us to form deep and meaningful connections with those around us.

At the same time, honesty can be a difficult thing to practice. We may be afraid of hurting the people we care about or of facing potential consequences for our actions. But the reality is that being honest is almost always the best choice, even if it is difficult in the moment.

One of the primary benefits of honesty in relationships is that it allows us to build trust with others. When we are honest about our thoughts, feelings, and experiences, we are showing others that we value their trust and that we are committed to building a strong and healthy relationship with them. This can lead to a deeper sense of connection and understanding between people, as well as a greater sense of intimacy and closeness.

Another benefit of honesty in relationships is that it allows us to resolve conflicts in a healthy and productive way. When we are honest with others about our concerns and grievances, we create a space in which we can work together to find a solution that works for everyone. This can be a difficult process, and it may involve compromise and difficult conversations, but it is always better than letting resentment and anger build up over time.

In addition to its benefits in relationships, honesty is also incredibly important in communication. When we communicate honestly with others, we are able to build stronger and more effective relationships in both our personal and professional lives. Honest communication allows us to establish clear expectations and boundaries with others, which can help to prevent misunderstandings and miscommunications in the future.

Moreover, honest communication allows us to be more productive and efficient in our interactions with others. When we are honest about our needs and goals, we are better able to work together with others to achieve our objectives. This can be especially important in professional settings, where clear communication and collaboration are essential to success.

However, it is important to remember that honesty does not mean that we should be rude or insensitive with others. There is a way to communicate honestly and respectfully, without sacrificing our own needs or the needs of others. When we practice honesty in a way that is empathetic and compassionate, we are better able to build

strong and healthy relationships with those around us.
the benefits of honesty in relationships and communication are numerous. When we are honest with ourselves and with others, we create a space of trust and understanding that allows us to form deep and meaningful connections with those around us. Honest communication allows us to establish clear expectations and boundaries, which can help to prevent misunderstandings and miscommunications in the future. By embracing honesty and practicing it in a way that is respectful and compassionate, we can build strong and healthy relationships that last a lifetime.

Communication and Honesty: The Key to Building Healthy Relationships

Healthy relationships are built on a foundation of open and honest communication. Whether it's a romantic partnership, a friendship, or a professional collaboration, effective communication and honesty are essential to building trust and fostering meaningful connections with others.

One of the primary benefits of honest communication is that it allows us to establish clear expectations and boundaries with others. When we communicate honestly, we are able to express our needs, desires, and concerns in a way that is clear and direct. This, in turn, enables us to work with others to develop a mutually beneficial arrangement that meets the needs of everyone involved.

Moreover, honest communication helps to prevent misunderstandings and miscommunications in the future. By being open and honest with others, we reduce the likelihood of misinterpretation and ambiguity, which can lead to unnecessary conflict and tension. Honest communication allows us to build a shared understanding of each other's perspectives, which can ultimately lead to greater cooperation and productivity in our relationships.

At the same time, honesty can be difficult to practice. We may be afraid of hurting the people we care about or of facing potential consequences for our actions. But the reality is that being honest is almost always the best choice, even if it is difficult in the moment.

Furthermore, honest communication fosters a deeper sense of intimacy and trust in our relationships. When we share our thoughts and feelings with others, we demonstrate that we value their trust and are committed to building a strong and healthy relationship with them. This can lead to a deeper sense of connection and understanding between people, as well as a greater sense of intimacy and closeness.

However, it's important to remember that honesty should be tempered with kindness and compassion. Being honest does not give us license to be rude or insensitive with others. When we practice honesty in a way that is empathetic and respectful, we are better able to build strong and healthy relationships with those around us.

In fact, communication and honesty go hand in hand in building healthy relationships. Effective communication requires honesty and transparency, and it also requires active listening and an open mind. When we communicate with others in an honest and respectful way, we create a safe and supportive space in which we can share our thoughts and feelings with one another without fear of judgment or retribution.

Moreover, honest communication is essential to maintaining the health and longevity of our relationships.

Over time, relationships can evolve and change, and it's important to communicate regularly with our loved ones in order to stay connected and attuned to their needs. By communicating honestly and openly, we can ensure that our relationships remain strong and vibrant, even in the face of challenges and obstacles.

communication and honesty are the key to building healthy relationships. Honest communication allows us to establish clear expectations and boundaries, prevent misunderstandings and miscommunications, and foster a deeper sense of intimacy and trust with others. By embracing honesty and practicing it in a way that is respectful and empathetic, we can build strong and lasting relationships that enrich our lives and the lives of those around us.

THE CONSEQUENCES OF DISHONESTY

CHAPTER THREE

THE CONSEQUENCES OF DISHONESTY

Dishonesty can have significant consequences on both a personal and societal level. When we are dishonest, we risk losing the trust and respect of those around us, and may also experience feelings of guilt and shame. Moreover, the effects of dishonesty can extend far beyond our immediate social circles, potentially leading to widespread harm and damage.

One of the most significant consequences of dishonesty is the erosion of trust. When we are caught in a lie, we betray the trust of others and can cause them to question our character and motives. This can have long-lasting effects on our relationships, both personal and professional, as trust is essential to building strong and meaningful connections with others. Once trust is lost, it can be difficult to regain, and we may find ourselves isolated and alone as a result of our dishonesty.

Moreover, dishonesty can also have significant impacts on our own mental health and well-being. When we lie, we may experience feelings of guilt and shame, which can lead to anxiety, depression, and other negative emotions. Over time, the stress and strain of maintaining a false facade can take a toll on our mental and physical health, leading to increased levels of stress and even illness.

On a societal level, the consequences of dishonesty can be even more severe. In politics, for example, dishonesty can lead to a breakdown of trust between citizens and their government, as well as increased polarization and division among different groups. When leaders lie or deceive, they risk eroding the very foundations of our democratic institutions, leading to increased corruption, unrest, and even violence.

Similarly, in business, dishonesty can have far-reaching consequences. When companies engage in fraudulent or deceptive practices, they risk not only losing the trust of their customers, but also facing legal action and financial ruin. Moreover, the effects of corporate dishonesty can extend to the broader economy, potentially leading to a loss of jobs and other negative consequences for individuals and communities.

In addition to the personal and societal consequences of dishonesty, it is also important to recognize the moral implications of our actions. When we are dishonest, we violate basic principles of ethics and morality, and may also compromise our own sense of self-worth and integrity. Moreover, by engaging in dishonest behavior, we may also contribute to a broader culture of mistrust and deception, perpetuating a cycle of negative behavior that can be difficult to break.

the consequences of dishonesty are far-reaching and significant. When we are dishonest, we risk losing the trust and respect of those around us, as well as experiencing negative emotional and physical effects. Moreover, the effects of dishonesty can extend far beyond our immediate social circles, potentially leading to widespread harm and damage. It is important, therefore, to cultivate a strong sense of integrity and honesty, both for our own benefit and for the greater good of society as a whole. By embracing the values of honesty, transparency, and accountability, we can build stronger and more meaningful relationships, and contribute to a more just and ethical world.

The impact of lying on personal and professional relationships

Lying is a common human behavior that can have significant impacts on both personal and professional relationships. Whether it is a white lie told to spare someone's feelings or a more significant deception, the effects of dishonesty can be far-reaching and long-lasting.

One example of the impact of lying on personal relationships can be seen in the story of Alex and Sam. Alex had been lying to Sam about his job for several months, telling him that he was working at a prestigious law firm when, in reality, he had been fired and was struggling to find a new job. At first, Alex thought that he was sparing Sam's feelings by hiding the truth, but as the lie continued to snowball, it began to take a toll on their relationship. Sam began to sense that something was off, and eventually confronted Alex about his job. When the truth finally came out, Sam was hurt and felt betrayed, leading to a breakdown in their relationship and a loss of trust that was difficult to repair.

Similarly, the impact of lying can also be seen in the workplace. For example, imagine a salesperson who lies to a potential customer about the quality of a product or service in order to make a sale. While this may result in short-term gains for the salesperson, it can have long-term consequences for the company and its relationships with customers. If the product or service does not live up to the customer's expectations, they may become dissatisfied and stop doing business with the company. Moreover, if the lie is discovered, it can lead to legal action, damaged reputations, and other negative consequences.

Another example of the impact of lying on personal relationships can be seen in the story of Laura and Mike. Laura had been lying to Mike about her past, telling him that she had grown up in a loving and stable family, when in reality she had a difficult and traumatic childhood. At first, Laura thought that she was protecting Mike by hiding the truth, but as their relationship grew more serious, she began to feel guilty and afraid that the truth would come out. When Mike eventually discovered the truth, he was hurt and felt that he had been deceived, leading to a breakdown in their relationship and a loss of trust that was difficult to repair.

Moreover, the impact of lying can extend far beyond individual relationships, with significant consequences for society as a whole. For example, imagine a politician who lies to the public in order to win an election. While this may result in short-term gains for the politician, it can have long-term consequences for the democratic process and the public's trust in government. If the lie is discovered, it can lead to a loss of trust in the political system, increased polarization and division, and even violence.

the impact of lying on personal and professional relationships can be significant and long-lasting. Whether it is a small white lie or a more significant deception, the effects of dishonesty can erode trust, damage reputations, and lead to the breakdown of relationships. It is important, therefore, to cultivate a strong sense of integrity and honesty, both for our own benefit and for the greater good of society as a whole. By embracing the values of honesty, transparency, and accountability, we can build stronger and more meaningful relationships, and contribute to a more just and ethical world.

"The Butterfly Effect of Lies: How Even Small Deceptions Can Wreak Havoc on Personal Relationships"

Lies are like pebbles thrown into a calm pond; they create ripples that extend far beyond the initial impact. Even seemingly small deceptions can have far-reaching consequences, and can ultimately cause irreparable damage to personal relationships. In this essay, we will explore the butterfly effect of lies, and how even small deceptions can wreak havoc on personal relationships.

Consider the story of Sarah and David. Sarah had been telling small lies to David for weeks, such as pretending to enjoy watching sports and exaggerating her interests to align more closely with David's. David, none the wiser, believed that he and Sarah shared many common interests, and he was excited about the potential for a long-term relationship. However, over time, the truth began to come out. Sarah's genuine interests started to shine through, and David realized that much of what he thought they had in common was a lie. The deception and dishonesty that Sarah had introduced into their relationship ultimately led to a breakdown in trust, and ultimately, the end of their relationship.

Furthermore, the butterfly effect of lies is not only confined to personal relationships but also extends to the professional world. Consider the story of John, who had been telling small lies to his boss about his qualifications and experience in order to get a promotion. Over time, John's lies began to catch up with him, and he found that he was unable to fulfill the expectations that came with his new position. This ultimately led to John's termination from the company, and a tarnished reputation in the industry.

The impact of small deceptions on personal relationships can also be seen in the story of Jenna and James. Jenna had been telling small lies to James for months, such as pretending to enjoy his company even when she didn't, and downplaying her emotions to avoid conflict. James, none the wiser, believed that their relationship was solid, and he was deeply in love with Jenna. However, over time, Jenna's dishonesty began to have an impact. James began to sense that something was off, and the trust that he had placed in Jenna began to erode. Eventually, the relationship ended, leaving both parties feeling hurt and betrayed.

The butterfly effect of lies can also have far-reaching consequences in the broader societal context. Consider the story of Mark, who had been telling small lies on social media in order to portray himself as more successful and happy than he really was. Over time, Mark's lies began to affect his mental health, as he struggled to maintain the facade that he had created. Moreover, Mark's dishonesty ultimately contributed to a broader cultural problem, as social media platforms became increasingly associated with superficiality and inauthenticity.

the butterfly effect of lies is a real and powerful force, capable of causing significant damage to personal relationships and broader social structures. Even small deceptions can create ripples that extend far beyond the initial impact, and can ultimately lead to a breakdown in trust, a loss of reputation, and irreparable harm to personal and professional relationships. It is important, therefore, to cultivate a strong sense of integrity and honesty, both for our own benefit and for the greater good of society as a whole. By embracing the values of honesty, transparency, and accountability, we can build stronger and more meaningful relationships, and contribute to a more just and ethical world.

"The High Cost of Dishonesty in the Workplace: Understanding the Impact of Lying on Professional Relationships"

Dishonesty in the workplace is a serious issue that can have significant consequences for individuals, teams, and entire organizations. From small lies to larger deceptions, dishonesty in the workplace can ultimately undermine trust, damage reputations, and jeopardize the success of a business. In this essay, we will explore the high cost of dishonesty in the workplace and the impact that lying can have on professional relationships.

Consider the story of Tom, who had been telling lies to his co-workers in order to make himself look better and get ahead in his career. Over time, Tom's lies began to have an impact on his team's productivity, as they found it difficult to work with someone who they could not trust. Moreover, Tom's dishonesty ultimately led to a loss of respect and a damaged reputation within the company. Eventually, Tom was let go, and he found it difficult to find another job due to the negative references from his former colleagues.

The high cost of dishonesty in the workplace can also be seen in the story of Jessica, who had been lying to her boss about her work hours in order to avoid being called out for underperformance. Over time, Jessica's dishonesty caught up with her, and she was unable to meet the expectations that came with her position. This ultimately led to her termination from the company, and a loss of reputation within the industry.

The impact of lying on professional relationships can also be seen in the story of Kevin and his team. Kevin had been telling lies to his team about the status of a major project, in order to avoid taking responsibility for missed deadlines and budget overruns. This ultimately led to a breakdown in communication, a loss of trust, and a significant setback for the company. Moreover, Kevin's dishonesty contributed to a broader culture of secrecy and lack of accountability within the company, ultimately making it more difficult to achieve their goals.

The high cost of dishonesty in the workplace can also have far-reaching consequences for broader societal structures. Consider the story of Robert, who had been lying about his qualifications and experience in order to secure a prestigious position at a major company. Over time, Robert's dishonesty began to have an impact on the company's reputation, as the quality of his work was not up to par. Moreover, Robert's dishonesty contributed to a broader culture of privilege and entitlement within the industry, making it more difficult for those without connections or privilege to succeed.

the high cost of dishonesty in the workplace is a serious issue that can have significant consequences for individuals, teams, and entire organizations. Dishonesty in the workplace can ultimately undermine trust, damage reputations, and jeopardize the success of a business. It is important, therefore, to cultivate a strong sense of integrity and honesty, both for our own benefit and for the greater good of society as a whole. By embracing the values of honesty, transparency, and accountability, we can build stronger and more successful businesses, and contribute to a more just and ethical world.

"The Ripple Effect of Lies: Exploring the Long-Term Consequences of Deception in Personal and Professional Relationships"

Deception and dishonesty in personal and professional relationships can have far-reaching consequences that go beyond the immediate impact of the lie itself. Like a stone thrown into a pond, a single act of deceit can create ripples that continue to expand outward, affecting not just the liar and the person lied to, but also those around them. In this essay, we will explore the ripple effect of lies and the long-term consequences of deception in personal and professional relationships.

Consider the story of Sarah and Jake, who had been in a committed relationship for several years. One day, Sarah discovered that Jake had been lying to her about his job, and had not been honest about his career prospects. Though Jake apologized and promised to change, Sarah found it difficult to trust him again. Over time, the effects of Jake's lies continued to affect their relationship, creating a sense of distance and mistrust that eventually led to their breakup.

The ripple effect of lies can also be seen in the story of Emily and her team. Emily had been lying to her colleagues about the status of a major project, in order to avoid taking responsibility for missed deadlines and budget overruns. Over time, this created a culture of secrecy and mistrust within the team, with each member feeling like they had to lie to cover up their mistakes. Ultimately, the project failed, and Emily's lies created a lasting sense of resentment and distrust among the team, affecting their ability to work together effectively in the future.

The long-term consequences of deception in personal and professional relationships can also be seen in the story of Michael, who had been lying to his colleagues about his qualifications and experience in order to secure a high-paying job. Though Michael's deception allowed him to achieve short-term success, over time, his lack of qualifications caught up with him, and he was eventually exposed. This led to a loss of reputation and damaged his ability to find future work.

The ripple effect of lies can also have a broader impact on society as a whole. Consider the story of Linda, who had been lying to her clients about the safety and effectiveness of her products, in order to boost sales. Over time, Linda's lies had far-reaching consequences, as the safety and effectiveness of her products were called into question. This ultimately led to a loss of trust in the industry, and a significant setback for companies that were genuinely trying to make a positive impact.

the ripple effect of lies is a powerful reminder of the long-term consequences of deception in personal and professional relationships. Lying can create a culture of mistrust and secrecy, and can ultimately undermine the very relationships we seek to build. It is important, therefore, to cultivate a strong sense of integrity and honesty, both for our own benefit and for the greater good of society as a whole. By embracing the values of honesty, transparency, and accountability, we can build stronger and more successful relationships, and contribute to a more just and ethical world.

"The Trust Paradox: Why Lying Can Be a Short-Term Solution with Long-Term Consequences in Relationships and the Workplace"

The act of lying can seem like a quick and easy solution to many problems. Whether it is to avoid getting in trouble, to spare someone's feelings, or to advance one's own interests, lying can sometimes seem like the best course of action in the moment. However, what many fail to consider is the long-term consequences that come with dishonesty. In relationships and the workplace, lying can create a trust paradox where short-term gains come at the cost of long-term consequences.

In personal relationships, lying can cause irreparable damage to the trust that has been built over time. For example, consider the case of Sarah, who lied to her partner about her whereabouts one night. Although the lie helped her avoid an argument with her partner in the moment, it created a rift in their trust that took months to repair. Her partner became increasingly suspicious of her actions and questioned her motives, leading to numerous arguments and a loss of trust that ultimately led to the end of their relationship.

In the workplace, lying can also have a negative impact on trust and can create a difficult paradox. For example, imagine a colleague who lies about their qualifications to get a promotion. While the lie may have led to short-term gains, it can lead to long-term consequences if the colleague is not able to perform the job effectively. This can cause the employer to lose trust in the employee, which can damage their professional reputation and limit future opportunities.

The trust paradox can also be seen in the case of companies that have lied to their customers or stakeholders. Consider the case of Volkswagen, which was caught lying about its emissions standards. The company's dishonesty led to a loss of trust and reputation, which ultimately led to a decline in sales and a loss of revenue.

While lying may seem like a quick and easy solution to many problems, the long-term consequences can be severe. When trust is broken, it can be difficult to repair, and can lead to negative outcomes in both personal and professional relationships. It is important to remember that honesty and transparency are the key to building and maintaining trust. In the long run, it is better to be honest and deal with the consequences of our actions, rather than to lie and risk damaging our relationships and reputations.

the trust paradox of lying is a reminder of the long-term consequences that come with dishonesty. While lying may seem like a quick solution in the short-term, it can ultimately damage our relationships and reputations. Honesty and transparency are the key to building and maintaining trust in both personal and professional relationships. By cultivating a culture of honesty and accountability, we can avoid the trust paradox and build stronger, more successful relationships in all aspects of our lives.

The long-term consequences of dishonesty

Dishonesty is often seen as an easy way out in the moment, a way to avoid negative consequences or to achieve short-term gains. However, the long-term consequences of dishonesty can be severe and far-reaching, affecting every aspect of our lives. From personal relationships to professional opportunities, dishonesty can lead to a loss of trust, reputation, and self-respect.

In personal relationships, the long-term consequences of dishonesty can be devastating. Whether it's lying about infidelity, hiding financial problems, or simply not being truthful about your feelings, dishonesty can erode the foundation of trust and intimacy that is necessary for a healthy relationship. Over time, the lies can become more and more difficult to keep up with, leading to a breakdown in communication and ultimately the dissolution of the relationship. Even if the truth eventually comes out, the damage may already be done, and the relationship may never fully recover.

In the workplace, the long-term consequences of dishonesty can be equally damaging. Lying to colleagues or superiors can damage your reputation and credibility, making it difficult to advance your career or secure new opportunities. If you are caught in a lie, you may face disciplinary action or even termination, which can have long-term financial and professional consequences. Even if you are not caught, the stress of keeping up the lie can lead to burnout, anxiety, and other negative effects on your mental and physical health.

The consequences of dishonesty can also extend beyond personal relationships and the workplace. For example, if you lie on a loan application or credit application, the consequences can be severe, including damage to your credit score, legal action, and even jail time. If you lie to friends or family, you may lose their trust and support, leading to feelings of isolation and loneliness.

It is important to remember that dishonesty can have long-term consequences that can be difficult to undo. The trust that is lost when we lie can take years to rebuild, and even then, it may never be fully restored. Over time, the weight of our lies can become heavier and heavier, leading to feelings of guilt, shame, and regret. These negative emotions can take a toll on our mental and physical health, leading to depression, anxiety, and other health issues.

The long-term consequences of dishonesty can also affect the way we see ourselves. When we lie, we are not being true to ourselves or living in alignment with our values. This can lead to feelings of self-doubt, self-criticism, and a lack of self-respect. In contrast, when we are honest, we feel a sense of integrity and self-respect, which can have positive effects on our mental and physical health, as well as our relationships and overall quality of life.

the long-term consequences of dishonesty can be severe and far-reaching, affecting every aspect of our lives. From personal relationships to professional opportunities, dishonesty can lead to a loss of trust, reputation, and self-respect. It is important to remember that honesty is the foundation of healthy relationships and a successful career. By cultivating a culture of honesty and accountability, we can avoid the long-term consequences of dishonesty and build stronger, more fulfilling lives for ourselves and those around us.

"The Slippery Slope of Dishonesty: How Small Lies Can Snowball into Major Consequences"

Dishonesty can often start small, with a little white lie or omission that seems harmless at the time. But what many people fail to realize is that even the smallest deception can snowball into major consequences. The slippery slope of dishonesty can lead to a loss of trust and damaged relationships, both personal and professional.

Consider the case of Mark and his girlfriend, Sarah. One day, Mark told Sarah that he had to work late at the office, when in fact, he went out with his friends for a few drinks. It seemed like a harmless lie, but Sarah soon found out the truth from one of Mark's co-workers. The lie made her feel betrayed and she started to question everything else Mark had ever told her. From that point on, their relationship was never the same, and Sarah found it hard to trust Mark.

In the workplace, a similar situation can occur. A small lie or deception, such as exaggerating the results of a project or taking credit for someone else's work, can lead to a loss of trust and respect from colleagues. For example, Alex worked hard on a presentation for his team, but his manager, Tom, took all the credit during the meeting with upper management. Alex felt betrayed and disrespected, and he lost respect for Tom. Over time, Alex's negative feelings towards Tom started to affect his work and his overall morale at the company.

Dishonesty can also have legal consequences. One example is the case of Enron, a company that went bankrupt in 2001 due to accounting fraud. The company's executives made false statements about the company's financial situation, which led to investors losing millions of dollars. The consequences of the dishonesty were devastating for everyone involved, including the employees who lost their jobs and the investors who lost their money.

The slippery slope of dishonesty is a dangerous path that can have long-lasting consequences. Even small lies or deceptions can lead to a loss of trust, damaged relationships, and legal ramifications. It's important to be honest, even when it's difficult, to avoid the potential snowball effect of dishonesty. In personal relationships, it's important to communicate openly and honestly, to avoid any misunderstandings that can lead to hurt feelings and a breakdown in trust. In the workplace, it's important to give credit where credit is due, to avoid damaging morale and relationships with colleagues. The consequences of dishonesty are far-reaching and can have a significant impact on every aspect of our lives.

"Liar, Liar: The Lasting Effects of Dishonesty on Personal Relationships"

Dishonesty can have lasting effects on personal relationships, both in the short-term and long-term. When someone lies to their partner, it can create feelings of hurt, betrayal, and distrust. Over time, these emotions can fester and lead to long-lasting problems in the relationship.

Take the case of Julie and Tom. Julie found out that Tom had been lying to her about his past, and she felt hurt and betrayed. Tom apologized, and at first, Julie was willing to forgive him. However, over time, she found that she couldn't let go of the feeling that she couldn't trust him. Every time Tom would tell her something, she would wonder if he was lying again. This lack of trust created a rift in their relationship, and ultimately, they decided to break up.

Dishonesty can also lead to a breakdown in communication. When one partner lies, it can make it difficult for the other partner to express their true feelings. This can lead to a lack of intimacy and connection in the relationship. For example, when Jake lied to his girlfriend, Maria, about where he was going one evening, Maria felt hurt and distant. She didn't feel like she could open up to him about her feelings, which led to a breakdown in communication between them.

The effects of dishonesty can also be seen in other types of relationships, such as friendships. When one friend lies to another, it can create feelings of hurt and mistrust. Over time, these negative feelings can cause the friendship to deteriorate. For example, when Sarah lied to her best friend, Alex, about something small, it led to a loss of trust. Alex started to question everything else that Sarah had ever told her, and eventually, their friendship fell apart.

The lasting effects of dishonesty can be difficult to overcome, but it is possible to rebuild trust and repair relationships. The first step is to acknowledge the hurt and betrayal that was caused by the dishonesty. The person who lied needs to take responsibility for their actions and apologize for any harm they caused. It's also important to be patient and understanding. Rebuilding trust takes time and effort, and it may not happen overnight.

Ultimately, the best way to avoid the lasting effects of dishonesty is to be honest and transparent in all of our relationships. When we are truthful with those around us, it builds a foundation of trust and mutual respect. Honesty is the key to strong, healthy relationships, and it's worth the effort to maintain it. By being honest and accountable for our actions, we can avoid the pain and lasting effects of dishonesty in our personal relationships.

"The Domino Effect of Deception: How Dishonesty Can Impact Every Aspect of Your Life"

Dishonesty is a destructive force that can wreak havoc on every aspect of your life. It can start small, with a little white lie here and there, but it has the potential to snowball into major consequences that can impact your personal relationships, professional life, and even your mental and emotional well-being.

At the root of dishonesty is often fear: fear of rejection, fear of consequences, or fear of not measuring up. But the consequences of lying can be far more detrimental than the temporary discomfort of telling the truth. Once you start down the path of deception, it can be difficult to turn back.

The impact of dishonesty is often a domino effect that spreads through every area of your life. When you lie to others, you erode trust and respect, which are essential components of healthy relationships. If people can't rely on you to tell the truth, they're unlikely to confide in you or trust you with important matters.

Over time, lying can also take a toll on your mental health. The guilt and anxiety that come with keeping up a façade can be overwhelming, and it can be easy to become consumed by the fear of being caught. This can lead to a constant state of stress and a loss of self-esteem, as you begin to doubt your own worth and the worth of your relationships.

In addition to personal relationships, dishonesty can have significant consequences in the workplace. When you lie to your colleagues or boss, you erode their trust in your abilities and your judgment. This can impact your ability to work collaboratively and can lead to missed opportunities for advancement or recognition.

The consequences of dishonesty can also extend to legal or financial repercussions. If your lies are discovered, it can damage your reputation and credibility, which can impact your ability to secure employment, loans, or other opportunities in the future. The impact can be long-lasting and can have a ripple effect on every area of your life.

The bottom line is that honesty is always the best policy. While it may be tempting to avoid discomfort in the short-term by telling a lie, the long-term consequences of dishonesty far outweigh any temporary relief. Building a reputation of honesty and trust takes time and effort, but it's essential for healthy relationships, personal well-being, and professional success.

It's never too late to start being honest with yourself and those around you. Even if you've made mistakes in the past, taking responsibility and making a commitment to truthfulness can be a powerful step towards building stronger relationships and a more fulfilling life.

"Beyond the Immediate: Understanding the Long-Term Consequences of Lying and Deceit"

We all tell lies from time to time. Sometimes it's to protect someone's feelings, or to get out of an uncomfortable situation. However, what many people don't realize is that even small lies can have long-term consequences that can impact every aspect of your life. The butterfly effect of deceit can be far-reaching and unpredictable, causing damage that is often difficult to repair.

One such example can be found in the story of a woman named Maria, who told a small lie to her best friend, Mary. Maria had promised to meet Mary for lunch, but at the last minute, she had a work emergency and had to cancel. Instead of telling Mary the truth, Maria said that she had a family emergency and had to leave town. Mary was sympathetic and understanding, and the two made plans to reschedule. However, over time, Maria found herself lying more and more frequently to avoid social situations or to get out of commitments. Eventually, Mary caught on to

Maria's dishonesty and ended their friendship. Maria was left feeling isolated and alone, with no one to turn to.

Similarly, in the workplace, lying can have a detrimental effect on professional relationships. A man named John was passed over for a promotion at work, and instead of accepting the decision and working harder to improve his performance, he lied to his boss, claiming that he had been unfairly overlooked and that a co-worker had taken credit for his work. The lie was eventually uncovered, and John was fired. Not only did he lose his job, but he also lost the respect of his colleagues, making it difficult for him to find new employment.

These stories demonstrate how even small lies can snowball into major consequences. Lies can erode trust, damage relationships, and create a web of deceit that is difficult to untangle. People who lie may think they are taking the easy way out, but in the long run, they often end up paying a high price.

In addition to damaging personal and professional relationships, lying can also have a negative impact on one's own self-esteem and self-worth. People who lie frequently may begin to question their own moral compass and feel guilty about their actions. This can lead to feelings of shame and isolation, further perpetuating the cycle of deception.

it's important to remember that honesty is always the best policy, even if it may be difficult in the moment. Small lies can quickly spiral out of control, causing damage that can be difficult to repair. Beyond the immediate consequences of lying, there are long-term effects that can impact every aspect of your life. By cultivating a culture of honesty and integrity, we can build stronger personal and professional relationships and live a more fulfilling life.

CULTIVATING A CULTURE OF HONESTY

CHAPTER FOUR

CULTIVATING A CULTURE OF HONESTY

Honesty is a fundamental value that is essential for building and maintaining healthy relationships, whether in personal or professional settings. It is the foundation upon which trust, respect, and integrity are built. However, it can be challenging to cultivate a culture of honesty in today's society, where lying and deceit are often normalized and even celebrated in popular media. Many people fear the consequences of telling the truth, whether it is being ostracized, criticized, or even losing their job. But the truth is, being honest is always the right thing to do, even if it is difficult or uncomfortable. Honesty not only promotes personal integrity and self-respect, but it also fosters positive self-image and helps create an environment where open communication and transparency are valued. In this essay, we will explore the importance of cultivating a culture of honesty, the challenges that can arise in doing so, and the benefits that can be gained for individuals, communities, and organizations. By examining realistic human behavior and incorporating real-life examples, we will explore how honesty can be an integral part of building and maintaining healthy relationships, and the steps that can be taken to foster a culture of honesty.

Creating an environment that encourages honesty

Creating an environment that encourages honesty is vital for individuals and organizations alike. Dishonesty can breed mistrust, damage relationships, and ultimately lead to negative consequences. Whether in personal relationships or professional settings, fostering a culture of honesty can bring numerous benefits, including improved communication, stronger relationships, and increased productivity. In this article, we will explore strategies for creating an environment that encourages honesty and the impact that this can have on individuals and organizations.

One key strategy for encouraging honesty is to create a safe space where individuals feel comfortable sharing their thoughts and feelings. This can be achieved by actively listening to others and ensuring that all voices are heard. When individuals feel that their opinions are valued and respected, they are more likely to be honest in their interactions. For example, in a work setting, creating an open-door policy where employees can speak freely with management can lead to a more transparent and honest environment.

Another strategy for building trust and fostering transparency is to lead by example. This means demonstrating honesty and integrity in all interactions and making it clear that these values are important. When leaders model honesty and transparency, it creates a culture where these values are expected and reinforced. For example, in a personal relationship, being honest about your own mistakes and shortcomings can encourage your partner to be honest as well.

Effective communication is also critical for fostering honesty. This means being clear and direct in your interactions, avoiding ambiguity or deception, and actively seeking feedback. When individuals feel that they can communicate openly and honestly, they are more likely to be honest in return. For example, in a team setting, encouraging open and honest communication can help identify potential problems early on and prevent them from becoming more significant issues.

Creating a sense of accountability is another critical strategy for building trust and fostering honesty. This means establishing clear expectations and holding individuals responsible for their actions. When individuals understand that their behavior has consequences, they are more likely to be honest in their interactions. For example, in a school setting, setting clear expectations for academic integrity and holding students accountable for plagiarism can help prevent dishonest behavior.

Finally, addressing the root causes of dishonesty is essential for creating an environment that encourages honesty. This means understanding the reasons why individuals may feel compelled to be dishonest and addressing these underlying issues. For example, in a work setting, high levels of stress or pressure to perform can lead to dishonesty, so creating a supportive work environment that prioritizes employee well-being can help reduce dishonest behavior.

creating an environment that encourages honesty is vital for building strong personal and professional relationships. By actively listening, leading by example, communicating effectively, establishing accountability, and addressing the root causes of dishonesty, individuals and organizations can create a culture of honesty and transparency that leads to positive outcomes. By valuing honesty and integrity in all interactions, we can create a world where honesty is the norm, and individuals can thrive both personally and professionally.

"Building Trust: The Role of Communication and Transparency in Cultivating Honesty in the Workplace"

Building trust is crucial in creating an environment that encourages honesty in the workplace. It is important for employees to feel that they can be honest with their superiors and colleagues without fear of retaliation or negative consequences. Trust is the foundation upon which healthy and effective relationships are built, both personally and professionally. Without trust, communication can become strained and workplace morale can suffer.

One way to build trust is through effective communication. Regular and transparent communication between managers and employees is essential to building trust. Managers should be open and approachable, listening to employees' concerns and addressing them in a timely and respectful manner. When employees feel that their voices are heard and their opinions matter, they are more likely to be honest and forthcoming.

Transparency is another key component in building trust. It is important for managers to be transparent in their decision-making processes, and to provide clear explanations for the actions they take. Transparency can also be fostered by being open about the company's goals, policies, and performance. When employees feel that they have a clear understanding of what is expected of them and how their work contributes to the overall success of the company, they are more likely to be invested in their work and to be honest in their interactions with colleagues and superiors.

A story that exemplifies the importance of trust and transparency in the workplace involves a mid-sized marketing firm that was struggling with low employee morale and high turnover rates. The CEO recognized that employees felt disconnected from the company's goals and vision, and that there was a lack of transparency in the decision-making process. In an effort to address these issues, the CEO held a company-wide meeting to discuss the company's goals, performance, and vision for the future. He encouraged employees to ask questions and to provide feedback, and made it clear that he was open to suggestions for improvement.

Over time, the company implemented several changes based on employee feedback, such as increasing the number of team-building activities and offering more opportunities for professional development. The CEO also made a point to regularly communicate the company's performance and goals, and to provide clear explanations for any decisions that were made. As a result of these efforts, employee morale improved, turnover rates decreased, and the company saw an increase in productivity and profitability.

In addition to effective communication and transparency, it is important for managers to lead by example when it comes to honesty and integrity. Employees are more likely to be honest and trustworthy when they see their superiors exhibiting those traits as well. Managers should hold themselves to the same standards of honesty and transparency that they expect from their employees, and should be willing to admit when they make mistakes or need to correct course.

Overall, building an environment that encourages honesty requires a combination of effective communication, transparency, and leading by example. When employees feel that they can trust their superiors and colleagues, they are more likely to be honest and forthcoming. This can lead to increased productivity, higher morale, and a more positive work culture.

"Setting the Tone: How Leaders Can Create a Culture of Honesty Through their Words and Actions"

In any organization or community, leaders play a critical role in setting the tone and establishing the culture. One of the most important aspects of this culture is honesty. Leaders who prioritize honesty and transparency can create a work environment where individuals feel safe to speak their minds, share their opinions, and take risks without fear of retaliation. The creation of such an environment starts with leaders understanding and modeling honesty in their own behavior. Leaders must demonstrate a willingness to be vulnerable, admit mistakes, and communicate transparently.

For instance, imagine a team leader who makes a mistake during a project, but instead of owning up to it, tries to cover it up and shift the blame to others. This behavior creates a culture of fear and distrust among team members. In contrast, a leader who admits to their mistake, takes ownership, and works with their team to correct it, will foster a culture of trust and collaboration.

Another key factor in creating an environment that encourages honesty is open communication. Leaders must establish channels of communication that encourage feedback and foster dialogue. They should be receptive to feedback and make themselves available for discussion. They should also ensure that team members have access to the information they need to make informed decisions.

For instance, consider a CEO who consistently communicates the company's goals and objectives with their employees, keeps them informed of important developments, and encourages them to share their thoughts and ideas. This CEO creates a culture of transparency, which allows employees to feel valued and connected to the organization.

In addition to these individual efforts, leaders can also implement policies and procedures that support honesty and transparency. This may include establishing a whistleblower hotline, providing training on ethical behavior, and implementing systems for anonymous reporting. These measures can help employees feel safe to report any concerns without fear of retaliation, thus increasing the likelihood of addressing issues before they become major problems.

For instance, imagine an organization that establishes a hotline where employees can anonymously report any violations of the code of conduct. This type of policy would encourage employees to speak up without fear of retaliation and allow the organization to address any ethical concerns before they escalate.

creating an environment that encourages honesty requires a multifaceted approach. Leaders must model honesty and transparency, establish open communication channels, and implement policies that support ethical behavior. When leaders prioritize honesty and transparency, they create a work environment where employees feel valued, connected, and invested in the success of the organization. "Breaking the Cycle of Dishonesty: Strategies for Encouraging Honesty in Personal Relationships"

In any relationship, honesty is the foundation upon which trust is built. However, it can be challenging to maintain honesty at all times, especially when it involves difficult or uncomfortable conversations. It's essential to remember that even small lies or omissions can lead to the erosion of trust and long-term consequences. Therefore, breaking the cycle of dishonesty requires a concerted effort from both parties involved.

The first step in encouraging honesty in personal relationships is to create an environment of safety and openness. Both parties must feel comfortable expressing their thoughts and feelings, even if they may be challenging to hear. One way to do this is to establish clear boundaries and communication guidelines. For instance, agreeing to avoid blame and judgment, using "I" statements, and listening actively can make difficult conversations more comfortable and productive.

Another critical strategy for fostering honesty is to lead by example. It is crucial to be honest in your communication and actions, even if it may be uncomfortable or awkward at times. When your partner sees you being truthful and open, it sets a positive example that can help to reinforce the value of honesty in the relationship.

It's also essential to address any instances of dishonesty promptly. When a lie is uncovered, it's natural to feel hurt and angry, but it's essential to resist the urge to retaliate with lies of your own. Instead, address the issue head-on by calmly and clearly communicating your feelings and concerns. By acknowledging the dishonesty, you can take steps towards rebuilding trust and moving forward.

Finally, it's important to remember that honesty is a continuous process that requires ongoing effort and attention. Regular check-ins and discussions can help to identify areas of improvement and ensure that both parties are feeling heard and valued. It's essential to approach these conversations with an open mind and a willingness to work towards solutions that benefit both parties.

creating an environment that encourages honesty requires a commitment to open communication, leading by example, prompt and clear resolution of instances of dishonesty, and ongoing effort to maintain transparency and trust. By embracing these strategies, both parties can work together to break the cycle of dishonesty and foster a relationship built on mutual trust and respect.

"Fostering a Sense of Accountability: How Creating Clear Expectations Can Encourage Honesty in Communities and Organizations"

In any community or organization, honesty is a crucial element for success. It builds trust and encourages transparency, which, in turn, creates a culture of accountability. When people are held accountable for their actions, they are more likely to act with integrity and honesty. However, fostering a sense of accountability can be challenging, particularly in large organizations or communities where people have varying levels of responsibility and influence.

One strategy for encouraging honesty and accountability is by creating clear expectations. This can be achieved through various means, such as creating a code of ethics, mission statement, or job descriptions that outline expectations for behavior and performance. By setting clear expectations, individuals are more likely to understand what is expected of them and feel a sense of responsibility to uphold those expectations.

Another way to foster accountability is by promoting a culture of transparency. This means being open and honest about decisions and actions, even when they may not be popular. When leaders model this behavior, it sends a message to others that honesty is valued and expected. This can lead to a snowball effect where individuals feel comfortable being honest and transparent, which in turn fosters a culture of accountability.

In addition, providing feedback is also an effective strategy for encouraging honesty and accountability. This involves providing constructive criticism and recognition for achievements, which can motivate individuals to be honest about their shortcomings and successes. By recognizing individuals for their achievements, it reinforces the value of honesty and accountability.

However, it is important to remember that creating a culture of accountability is not a one-time effort. It requires ongoing effort and attention to maintain. Leaders and individuals must continue to model honesty and transparency in their daily actions and behaviors, and the culture must be reinforced through continuous training, communication, and feedback.

fostering a sense of accountability through clear expectations, transparency, and feedback can create a culture of honesty and integrity in organizations and communities. This leads to greater trust, collaboration, and ultimately, success.

Strategies for building trust and fostering transparency

Trust and transparency are essential components for building strong relationships, whether it's in the workplace, personal relationships, or within communities. Trust is the foundation on which relationships are built, and without it, it can be challenging to establish meaningful and lasting connections. In today's fast-paced and competitive world, building trust and fostering transparency has become more important than ever before. Here are some strategies for building trust and fostering transparency.

The first step in building trust and fostering transparency is to communicate openly and honestly. Communication is key to any successful relationship, and it is essential to establish open lines of communication to build trust. People need to feel that they can communicate their thoughts and feelings without fear of judgement or retribution. Encouraging open and honest communication can lead to a more transparent and trusting environment, allowing individuals to build stronger connections and relationships.

The second strategy for building trust and fostering transparency is to lead by example. Leaders play a critical role in establishing a culture of transparency and trust within organizations. By modeling honest and ethical behavior, leaders can set the tone for their employees to follow. Leaders who demonstrate integrity and accountability can create a safe space for their employees to communicate openly and honestly. This creates a culture where transparency is valued, and trust is built over time.

The third strategy for building trust and fostering transparency is to provide regular feedback. Regular feedback is essential for building trust and fostering transparency in the workplace. Feedback can help individuals understand their strengths and weaknesses and provide insight into how they can improve. When individuals receive feedback on their performance, they are more likely to feel valued and supported. This, in turn, can lead to increased trust and transparency within the organization.

The fourth strategy for building trust and fostering transparency is to be consistent. Consistency is critical in establishing trust and fostering transparency. When individuals know what to expect, they are more likely to feel comfortable communicating openly and honestly. Consistency in communication, behavior, and decision-making can create a sense of predictability and stability that fosters trust and transparency.

building trust and fostering transparency is crucial for developing strong relationships in both personal and professional settings. Strategies such as open and honest communication, leading by example, providing regular feedback, and being consistent can help individuals establish a culture of honesty and accountability. These strategies require effort and commitment, but the benefits of building trust and fostering transparency are significant, including increased collaboration, productivity, and overall satisfaction. By focusing on these strategies, individuals can create environments where trust and transparency thrive, leading to meaningful and lasting relationships.

"From the Ground Up: How Transparency and Communication Can Build Trust in Organizational Settings"

Building trust in any organization is a critical component of its success. When employees, customers, and other stakeholders trust the organization, they are more likely to support it, remain loyal, and feel invested in its success. Trust is built on a foundation of transparency and communication, which can create a culture that encourages honesty and fosters positive relationships.

The first step in building a culture of transparency is to establish clear and open lines of communication. This means that employees need to feel comfortable speaking up about their ideas, concerns, and feedback. Leaders should create an environment where employees feel comfortable sharing their thoughts without fear of repercussions. Regular meetings, both one-on-one and in groups, can provide opportunities for employees to communicate with their leaders and peers, ask questions, and share their perspectives.

Transparency is also essential to building trust in an organization. This means that leaders need to be open and honest about the decisions they make and the reasoning behind them. They should share information about the company's financial health, its plans for growth, and any challenges it is facing. When leaders are transparent about these issues, employees can better understand the organization's goals and feel invested in its success.

Another way to build trust and foster transparency is by providing employees with opportunities to provide feedback. This can be done through surveys, focus groups, or suggestion boxes, for example. When employees feel that their voices are heard and their opinions matter, they are more likely to feel invested in the organization and its success.

Finally, it is essential to follow through on commitments and promises. When leaders make promises to employees, customers, or other stakeholders, they must keep them. Failure to do so can damage trust and credibility. Leaders should set realistic expectations and be transparent about any challenges that may arise in meeting those expectations. This can help build trust and foster transparency by demonstrating that leaders are willing to be honest about their limitations and challenges.

Overall, building trust and fostering transparency in an organization requires ongoing effort and commitment. It is not a one-time event, but a continual process. By establishing clear and open lines of communication, being transparent about decision-making and plans, providing opportunities for feedback, and following through on commitments, leaders can create a culture that encourages honesty and fosters positive relationships. When organizations cultivate a culture of transparency and trust, they are more likely to succeed and thrive in the long run.

"Starting with Yourself: Strategies for Building Trust and Fostering Transparency in Personal Relationships"

Building trust and fostering transparency are essential for any healthy relationship. Whether it's with a friend, family member, or romantic partner, trust and transparency lay the foundation for a strong connection built on mutual respect and honesty. But it's not always easy to know where to start or how to begin building these qualities in a relationship. One strategy for building trust and fostering transparency is to start with yourself.

Being honest with yourself and acknowledging your own values, beliefs, and desires can help you better understand what you need from a relationship and how to communicate those needs to others. It also sets an example for those around you, showing them that you prioritize honesty and transparency. When you lead with honesty and transparency, you create a safe space for others to follow suit.

Another strategy for building trust and fostering transparency is to practice active listening. Listening without judgment and with an open mind creates a space for the other person to be vulnerable and honest. By actively listening, you show that you care about what the other person has to say and that you're willing to put in the effort to understand their perspective. This can help the other person feel heard and validated, which builds trust and encourages honesty.

Being clear and direct in your communication is also important for building trust and fostering transparency. By expressing your needs and feelings clearly, you help avoid miscommunication and ensure that both parties are on the same page. This allows for a deeper level of understanding and helps to build trust between individuals.

Another key strategy for building trust and fostering transparency is to be accountable for your actions. When you make a mistake or do something that negatively impacts the other person, owning up to it and taking responsibility can show that you're committed to being honest and transparent in the relationship. It also shows that you respect the other person enough to be honest with them, even when it's difficult.

In order to build trust and foster transparency in any relationship, it's important to prioritize open and honest communication. This means being willing to share your thoughts and feelings, as well as actively listening to the thoughts and feelings of others. It also means being accountable for your actions and demonstrating a commitment to transparency and honesty. By setting an example through your own behavior and prioritizing these qualities in your relationships, you can help create a culture of trust and transparency that will benefit everyone involved.

"Tools for Success: Practical Strategies for Fostering Trust and Transparency in the Workplace"

Trust and transparency are two critical components of a successful workplace. When employees trust their leaders and coworkers, they are more likely to collaborate effectively, communicate openly, and take risks that lead to innovation and growth. However, building trust and fostering transparency can be a challenging task, particularly in environments where competition is high, or communication is limited. Fortunately, there are several practical strategies that leaders and employees can employ to cultivate trust and transparency in the workplace.

Firstly, one of the most effective strategies for building trust and transparency in the workplace is to establish clear expectations and goals. When everyone on the team knows what they are working towards and what is expected of them, they are more likely to be accountable for their actions, and less likely to engage in behavior that is detrimental to the team's success. By communicating expectations and goals, leaders can create a shared vision that inspires collaboration and fosters a sense of purpose among team members.

Another important strategy for fostering trust and transparency is to encourage open communication. Leaders who listen to feedback, are willing to admit their mistakes, and take the time to understand their employees' concerns, are more likely to build strong relationships with their teams. Additionally, providing opportunities for employees to share their opinions and ideas can help to cultivate a sense of ownership and investment in the organization's success.

Moreover, providing opportunities for learning and growth is another effective way to foster trust and transparency in the workplace. When employees feel that they are valued and that their contributions are recognized, they are more likely to take an active interest in the organization's goals and objectives. Leaders can create opportunities for professional development, training, and mentorship, which not only helps employees develop new skills but also signals that the organization is invested in their success.

Finally, it is essential to create a workplace culture that prioritizes integrity, respect, and fairness. Leaders who model ethical behavior, communicate openly and honestly, and treat employees with respect are more likely to build trust and foster a sense of transparency in the workplace. Moreover, it is crucial to establish systems that promote fairness and equity, such as performance evaluations that are objective and transparent, and compensation and rewards systems that are based on merit and achievement.

building trust and fostering transparency is critical to the success of any organization. By establishing clear expectations and goals, encouraging open communication, providing opportunities for learning and growth, and creating a workplace culture that prioritizes integrity, respect, and fairness, leaders can create an environment that encourages honesty, collaboration, and innovation. Moreover, when employees trust their leaders and coworkers, they are more likely to take risks that lead to growth and success, making it a win-win situation for everyone involved.

"Creating a Safe Space: Strategies for Encouraging Honesty and Transparency in Community and Group Settings"

Creating a safe space where honesty and transparency can thrive is essential for building strong communities and groups. Without open and honest communication, misunderstandings can arise, trust can erode, and relationships can break down. Therefore, it is important to develop strategies that encourage honesty and transparency in community and group settings.

One of the most important strategies for creating a safe space is to establish clear expectations around communication and behavior. This can be achieved by setting ground rules that everyone agrees to follow. For example, in a group setting, participants may agree to speak honestly, listen actively, and respect each other's opinions. By setting these expectations from the outset, everyone is clear on what is expected of them and how they can contribute to a positive and respectful environment.

Another key strategy for encouraging honesty and transparency is to lead by example. As a leader or facilitator, it is important to model the behavior you want to see in others. This means being open and honest about your own thoughts and feelings, as well as acknowledging when you make mistakes. By demonstrating vulnerability and a willingness to be honest, you create a culture where others feel safe to do the same.

Active listening is also a crucial tool for fostering honesty and transparency in community and group settings. When people feel heard and understood, they are more likely to open up and share their thoughts and feelings. To be an effective listener, it is important to give your full attention to the speaker, ask open-ended questions, and avoid interrupting or judging them. By creating a supportive and non-judgmental environment, you can help people feel comfortable sharing their experiences and perspectives.

Establishing a feedback loop is another effective strategy for encouraging honesty and transparency in community and group settings. This can be achieved by regularly soliciting feedback from participants, whether through surveys, focus groups, or one-on-one conversations. By actively seeking feedback, you show that you value the opinions and perspectives of everyone in the group, which can encourage people to be more open and honest in their communication.

Finally, it is important to remember that building a culture of honesty and transparency is an ongoing process. It requires regular check-ins, open communication, and a willingness to adapt and change as needed. By consistently reinforcing the importance of honesty and transparency, and by providing the necessary support and resources, you can create a safe space where everyone feels comfortable sharing their thoughts and feelings, and where trust and relationships can thrive.

DEVELOPING SELF-AWARENESS

CHAPTER FIVE
DEVELOPING SELF-AWARENESS
 Developing self-awareness is a key component of personal growth and development. It is the ability to recognize one's own thoughts, emotions, and behaviors and how they impact the people and the world around us. Self-awareness is a powerful tool that can help individuals understand their strengths and weaknesses, improve their relationships, and navigate life's challenges with more ease and confidence.

Self-awareness is not something that can be developed overnight. It is a journey that requires ongoing effort and a willingness to be open and honest with oneself. It involves taking a step back from the constant noise and distractions of everyday life to reflect on one's inner world and examine the patterns of thoughts and behaviors that have become deeply ingrained over time.

Developing self-awareness requires a commitment to personal growth and a willingness to confront the parts of ourselves that we may not like or want to acknowledge. It is not always easy, but the benefits are worth the effort. By developing self-awareness, individuals can gain a deeper understanding of themselves, build stronger relationships with others, and create a more fulfilling and meaningful life.

In this article, we will explore the importance of self-awareness and provide practical tips and strategies for developing self-awareness in daily life. We will look at the impact of self-awareness on personal growth, relationships, and career success, and explore the challenges that can arise when we avoid or suppress our inner world. Through the lens of realistic human behavior and real-life examples, we will examine the benefits of developing self-awareness and the positive impact it can have on our lives.

Recognizing and addressing personal biases and limiting beliefs

 Recognizing and addressing personal biases and limiting beliefs is a crucial step in developing self-awareness. Our biases and beliefs are shaped by our experiences, upbringing, and societal norms. They can be conscious or unconscious, and they can impact the way we interact with others and make decisions. To truly understand ourselves and our place in the world, we must examine these biases and beliefs, and be open to changing them.

For example, Emma had always believed that people who are successful in their careers are naturally talented and confident. She struggled with self-doubt and often felt inadequate in her own job. However, after attending a leadership development program, Emma began to recognize that her belief was limiting her own potential. She started to challenge her thinking and began to actively seek out examples of people who achieved success through hard work and perseverance. This allowed her to reframe her beliefs and increase her own confidence and sense of self-worth.

Similarly, Jack had always been taught that people who were different from him were to be feared. He held onto these beliefs until he met a coworker who challenged his thinking. Through conversation and exposure to different perspectives, Jack recognized that his belief was not based in reality, and that he had been missing out on the opportunity to learn from and connect with a diverse group of people. He started to actively work on addressing his biases and became a champion of diversity and inclusion in his workplace.

These stories demonstrate that recognizing and addressing personal biases and limiting beliefs is not only important for personal growth, but it also has a positive impact on the people around us. When we are aware of our own biases and beliefs, we are more empathetic, open-minded, and better able to connect with others.

However, it's not always easy to recognize our own biases and beliefs. They can be deeply ingrained and we may not even realize that they exist. It takes courage and vulnerability to examine our own thinking and challenge our beliefs. It's important to create a safe and supportive environment where people feel comfortable exploring their biases and beliefs.

Organizations and communities can play a role in creating this type of environment. They can provide training and resources to help people recognize and address their biases, and they can promote diversity and inclusion to encourage people to connect with those who are different from them. In addition, they can create spaces for dialogue and reflection, where people can openly share their experiences and perspectives.

recognizing and addressing personal biases and limiting beliefs is a critical step in developing self-awareness. It requires us to be open to changing our thinking, and to actively challenge the beliefs that may be holding us back. When we do this work, we not only grow personally, but we create a more inclusive and empathetic world.

The Importance of Self-Reflection: How to Identify and Challenge Personal Biases and Limiting Beliefs

Self-reflection is an essential tool in developing self-awareness and challenging personal biases and limiting beliefs. Biases and limiting beliefs are beliefs and attitudes that we hold about ourselves, others, and the world around us. They are often unconscious, and can stem from past experiences, cultural and societal influences, and personal values and assumptions. These biases and beliefs can impact our decision-making, relationships, and perceptions, and may even limit our potential for growth and success.

Self-reflection involves taking the time to examine our thoughts, feelings, and actions in a non-judgmental way, with the goal of gaining a better understanding of ourselves and our beliefs. This can be a challenging process, as it requires us to be honest with ourselves and confront aspects of our identity and experiences that we may have been avoiding or denying.

One way to begin the process of self-reflection is to ask ourselves questions that encourage introspection and self-awareness. These questions may include: What do I believe about myself, others, and the world around me? How have my past experiences influenced my beliefs and attitudes? Am I holding on to any beliefs or attitudes that are limiting my potential or preventing me from seeing things clearly? What steps can I take to challenge and change these beliefs and attitudes?

Another important aspect of self-reflection is recognizing when our biases and limiting beliefs are impacting our behavior and interactions with others. This can be particularly challenging when our biases and beliefs are deeply ingrained, and we may not even realize that they are influencing our thoughts and actions. However, by taking the time to examine our own behavior and the way we interact with others, we can begin to identify patterns and areas where our biases and beliefs may be impacting our relationships and decision-making.

In order to address personal biases and limiting beliefs, it is important to develop strategies for challenging and changing these beliefs. This may involve seeking out new information and perspectives, engaging in dialogue with others who hold different beliefs, and actively working to challenge our own assumptions and biases. It may also involve seeking out support from others, such as friends, family, or professional counselors, who can help us to gain perspective and develop strategies for overcoming our biases and limiting beliefs.

By recognizing and addressing personal biases and limiting beliefs, we can develop a greater sense of self-awareness, build stronger and more authentic relationships with others, and open ourselves up to new opportunities and experiences. However, this process requires a commitment to ongoing self-reflection and a willingness to confront aspects of ourselves that may be uncomfortable or challenging. Ultimately, the rewards of developing self-awareness and challenging personal biases and limiting beliefs can be significant, both in our personal and professional lives.

Overcoming Obstacles: Strategies for Recognizing and Addressing Limiting Beliefs to Achieve Success

Limiting beliefs can hold people back from reaching their full potential and achieving success. These beliefs are often formed early in life and can stem from negative experiences, societal pressures, or even from well-meaning loved ones. Over time, these beliefs can become deeply ingrained, making them difficult to identify and overcome. However, by recognizing and addressing these limiting beliefs, individuals can break through the barriers that hold them back.

One of the first steps in overcoming limiting beliefs is to identify them. This requires self-reflection and an honest examination of one's own thoughts and behaviors. It may be helpful to keep a journal or make a list of the negative beliefs that come to mind when thinking about one's goals and aspirations. Some common limiting beliefs include the idea that success is only for the lucky or the wealthy, that failure is inevitable, or that one's abilities are fixed and cannot be improved.

Once these limiting beliefs have been identified, it is important to challenge them. This involves questioning the validity of the belief and looking for evidence to support or refute it. For example, if the belief is that success is only for the lucky, one could look for examples of people who have achieved success through hard work and perseverance rather than luck. By challenging these beliefs, individuals can begin to see that they are not necessarily true, and that there may be other, more positive ways of looking at the situation.

Another strategy for overcoming limiting beliefs is to reframe them in a more positive light. For example, instead of thinking "I'm not smart enough to succeed in this field," one could reframe the belief as "I may not know everything now, but I am capable of learning and improving." By reframing limiting beliefs in this way, individuals can begin to see them as opportunities for growth and development, rather than as insurmountable obstacles.

Finally, it is important to surround oneself with supportive people who encourage personal growth and development. This may mean seeking out a mentor, joining a support group, or simply spending time with friends and family who are positive and encouraging. Having a supportive network can help individuals to stay motivated and focused on their goals, even in the face of challenges and setbacks.

recognizing and addressing personal biases and limiting beliefs is an important step towards achieving success. By identifying these beliefs, challenging them, reframing them, and surrounding oneself with supportive people, individuals can break through the barriers that hold them back and reach their full potential. It is not always an easy process, but with self-reflection and a willingness to change, anyone can overcome their limiting beliefs and achieve their goals.

Dismantling Assumptions: Uncovering Personal Biases and Developing Self-Awareness for Improved Relationships

Developing self-awareness is essential for personal growth and improved relationships. One of the key aspects of self-awareness is recognizing and dismantling personal biases. We all have biases, whether conscious or unconscious, and they can impact our thoughts, feelings, and behaviors. To improve relationships, it is crucial to uncover and challenge these biases. This means becoming aware of the assumptions we make about others based on factors such as race, gender, sexual orientation, or religion.

One common bias is the tendency to make assumptions about a person's behavior based on stereotypes. For example, assuming that someone is untrustworthy because of their race or nationality. This bias can be particularly harmful in personal and professional relationships, as it can create misunderstandings and erode trust. To address this bias, it is important to consciously question assumptions and seek to understand the individual, rather than making assumptions based on group characteristics.

Another bias that can impact relationships is confirmation bias, which is the tendency to seek out information that confirms our existing beliefs and ignore evidence that contradicts them. This can lead to misunderstandings and arguments, particularly in situations where individuals hold different perspectives. To overcome confirmation bias, it is important to actively seek out information and perspectives that challenge our beliefs and remain open to the possibility that we may be wrong.

Limiting beliefs can also impact our self-awareness and relationships. These beliefs are negative thoughts and beliefs that we hold about ourselves, such as "I'm not good enough" or "I'll never be successful." Limiting beliefs can prevent us from taking risks, trying new things, and pursuing our goals. To overcome these beliefs, it is important to challenge them by examining the evidence that supports them and identifying evidence that contradicts them. This can help to develop a more realistic and positive self-image, which can improve self-esteem and confidence.

Developing self-awareness is an ongoing process, and it requires a willingness to examine our own biases and beliefs. It can be uncomfortable to confront our own limitations and biases, but it is necessary for personal growth and improved relationships. By actively seeking to recognize and dismantle personal biases, and challenging limiting beliefs, we can develop a stronger sense of self-awareness and build more positive and authentic relationships.

Getting Out of Your Own Way: Recognizing Personal Biases and Limiting Beliefs to Promote Personal Growth

Personal biases and limiting beliefs can significantly hinder an individual's personal growth and development. Often, people are their own biggest obstacle, and it can be challenging to recognize and overcome these limitations. The first step in getting out of your own way is recognizing that you have biases and beliefs that may be holding you back. This may require some deep self-reflection and a willingness to challenge your assumptions.

One common limiting belief is the idea that success is reserved for certain people or that achieving success requires a certain level of privilege or luck. This type of belief can lead to self-doubt and lack of motivation, as people may feel like they have no control over their success. However, it's essential to recognize that success is attainable for anyone who is willing to put in the effort and work towards their goals.

Another common personal bias is the tendency to see things in black and white, without considering the shades of gray in between. This can lead to narrow-minded thinking and an unwillingness to consider alternative perspectives. Recognizing this bias and being open to new ideas and different viewpoints can help broaden your perspective and promote personal growth.

Overcoming personal biases and limiting beliefs can be challenging, but it's important to remember that change is possible. A crucial step in this process is taking ownership of your thoughts and behaviors and being willing to challenge them. This may require seeking feedback from others, doing research, or practicing mindfulness and self-reflection.

It's also essential to surround yourself with a supportive community of people who share your values and can offer constructive criticism and support. This community can help hold you accountable and provide a sounding board for new ideas and perspectives.

recognizing and overcoming personal biases and limiting beliefs is critical to promoting personal growth and achieving success. By challenging assumptions and being open to new ideas, individuals can broaden their perspectives and cultivate a growth mindset. Surrounding oneself with a supportive community can also provide the motivation and accountability needed to overcome these obstacles and achieve personal growth.

The importance of self-reflection in building a foundation of truthfulness

Self-reflection is an essential tool for building a foundation of truthfulness in our lives. It allows us to examine our thoughts, beliefs, and actions, and gain a deeper understanding of ourselves. By taking the time to reflect on our experiences and behaviors, we can identify patterns and make changes that promote honesty and integrity.

In order to engage in self-reflection, we must be willing to honestly examine our thoughts and behaviors. This can be a difficult and uncomfortable process, as it requires us to confront our own flaws and limitations. However, it is important to remember that self-reflection is not about self-criticism, but rather about gaining insight and understanding.

One effective way to engage in self-reflection is through journaling. By writing down our thoughts and feelings, we can gain clarity and insight into our inner world. This process can help us identify patterns of behavior and thought that may be hindering our ability to be truthful with ourselves and others.

Another important aspect of self-reflection is taking responsibility for our actions. It is easy to blame external factors for our behavior, but ultimately, we are in control of our choices. By acknowledging our role in our experiences, we can take ownership and make changes that promote honesty and integrity.

Finally, self-reflection can also help us identify our values and priorities. When we have a clear understanding of what we stand for, we are better equipped to make decisions that align with our beliefs. This can help us build a foundation of truthfulness in all areas of our lives.

self-reflection is an essential tool for building a foundation of truthfulness in our lives. It allows us to examine our thoughts, beliefs, and actions, and gain a deeper understanding of ourselves. By taking responsibility for our actions, identifying patterns of behavior, and gaining clarity about our values, we can promote honesty and integrity in all aspects of our lives.

The Power of Self-Reflection: How Examining Our Thoughts and Behaviors Can Improve Self-Awareness and Honesty

Self-reflection is the process of examining one's own thoughts, emotions, and behaviors in order to gain a deeper understanding of oneself. It can be a powerful tool in building self-awareness and honesty, as it allows individuals to recognize and examine their own biases, assumptions, and limiting beliefs. By taking the time to reflect on our own experiences and actions, we can begin to identify patterns and areas for growth.

Through self-reflection, individuals can also gain a greater sense of clarity and purpose in their lives. By examining our goals and values, we can ensure that our actions align with our true desires and motivations. This can lead to a greater sense of fulfillment and happiness, as we are living authentically and in accordance with our own values.

However, self-reflection can also be a challenging and uncomfortable process. It requires individuals to confront their own weaknesses and vulnerabilities, which can be difficult and even painful. It can be tempting to avoid this discomfort, but doing so can ultimately lead to a lack of self-awareness and an inability to grow and improve.

One way to make self-reflection more manageable is to set aside dedicated time and space for it. This can be as simple as taking a few minutes each day to reflect on your experiences and emotions, or as involved as participating in a regular meditation or journaling practice. The important thing is to create a space where you can reflect without distraction or interruption.

Another key component of self-reflection is honesty. It is important to be honest with yourself about your thoughts, feelings, and behaviors, even if they are difficult to confront. This requires a willingness to be vulnerable and to acknowledge areas where you may be falling short. However, it is through this honesty that individuals can identify areas for growth and work towards improving themselves.

In addition, it can be helpful to seek feedback from others in order to gain a more well-rounded perspective. This can be done through seeking the input of trusted friends or family members, or through participating in a group or community that values honest and constructive feedback. By opening ourselves up to the insights and perspectives of others, we can gain a deeper understanding of ourselves and our place in the world.

Overall, self-reflection is an essential tool for building self-awareness and honesty. By taking the time to examine our own thoughts and behaviors, we can identify our own biases and limiting beliefs, and work towards becoming more authentic and aligned with our values. While it can be a challenging process, the benefits of self-reflection are profound and can lead to a greater sense of fulfillment, purpose, and happiness.

Breaking Down Barriers: Recognizing and Challenging Limiting Beliefs to Cultivate a Culture of Honesty

A culture of honesty is one where individuals feel comfortable expressing their thoughts and feelings, without fear of judgment or retribution. However, personal biases and limiting beliefs can create barriers that prevent individuals from being truthful and open. In order to cultivate a culture of honesty, it's important to recognize and challenge these barriers to honesty.

One common barrier to honesty is the fear of vulnerability. Many individuals are afraid of being judged or rejected for their thoughts or feelings, which can cause them to keep their thoughts and emotions to themselves. This fear of vulnerability can be especially strong in work environments, where there is often pressure to appear competent and in control. To break down this barrier, individuals must be willing to acknowledge their fears and take risks by being honest and open.

Another common barrier to honesty is the presence of personal biases. Everyone has biases, whether they are aware of them or not. These biases can lead individuals to make assumptions about others, and to overlook information that doesn't fit with their preconceived ideas. To overcome this barrier, individuals must be willing to examine their own biases and challenge their assumptions. By being open to different perspectives and considering all available information, individuals can cultivate a more accurate and honest understanding of the world around them.

Limiting beliefs can also be a barrier to honesty. These beliefs are often deeply ingrained and can prevent individuals from seeing new opportunities or taking risks. For example, an individual may believe that they are not smart enough to pursue a certain career or that they don't have the skills to succeed in a particular field. These beliefs can hold individuals back from pursuing their dreams and expressing themselves honestly. To overcome this barrier, individuals must be willing to challenge their limiting beliefs and explore new possibilities.

In order to break down these barriers to honesty, individuals must also be willing to engage in self-reflection.

By examining their thoughts, emotions, and behaviors, individuals can gain a deeper understanding of themselves and the factors that may be preventing them from being honest. This process can be challenging, as it requires individuals to be honest with themselves and acknowledge their flaws and weaknesses. However, it is also essential for personal growth and for cultivating a culture of honesty.

Ultimately, recognizing and challenging personal biases and limiting beliefs is essential for building a foundation of truthfulness. By breaking down these barriers to honesty, individuals can create a safe and open environment where everyone feels comfortable expressing their thoughts and emotions. This kind of culture of honesty can foster greater understanding and collaboration, leading to increased creativity, productivity, and overall satisfaction.

Unpacking Personal Biases: Strategies for Identifying and Addressing Our Preconceived Notions to Foster Truthfulness

Personal biases are deeply ingrained beliefs or opinions that we hold about certain people, groups, or situations. They are often formed through our personal experiences, cultural or societal influences, and can be unconscious or conscious. These biases can affect our thoughts, behaviors, and decisions, and may even prevent us from recognizing the truth. Therefore, identifying and addressing personal biases is essential for building a foundation of truthfulness in our interactions with others.

The first step in recognizing and addressing personal biases is to become aware of them. This involves examining our thoughts, beliefs, and actions, and identifying any patterns or inconsistencies that may indicate the presence of a bias. For example, we may find ourselves making assumptions about someone's abilities based on their gender or race, or feeling uncomfortable around people who have different political views than our own. By becoming aware of these biases, we can take steps to challenge them and prevent them from influencing our actions.

One effective strategy for challenging personal biases is to seek out new perspectives and experiences. This involves intentionally exposing ourselves to people, cultures, and situations that are different from our own, and being open to learning from them. For example, if we hold a bias against a particular group of people, we may seek out opportunities to interact with members of that group, read books or articles written by members of that group, or participate in events or activities that are popular among that group. By exposing ourselves to these new perspectives, we can challenge our preconceived notions and develop a more accurate and nuanced understanding of the world around us.

Another important strategy for addressing personal biases is to actively listen to others. This means paying attention to the words and behaviors of those around us, and being willing to accept feedback and criticism. By listening to the perspectives of others, we can gain a better understanding of their experiences and perspectives, and identify any biases that we may be holding. Additionally, by accepting feedback and criticism, we can learn from our mistakes and develop a more accurate and truthful view of the world.

Finally, it is important to develop a practice of self-reflection in order to identify and address personal biases. This involves regularly examining our thoughts, behaviors, and actions, and assessing whether they align with our values and beliefs. By reflecting on our own experiences and behaviors, we can identify any biases that may be influencing our decisions, and take steps to address them. This can involve seeking out the opinions of others, challenging our own assumptions, and actively working to change our thoughts and behaviors.

recognizing and addressing personal biases is essential for building a foundation of truthfulness in our interactions with others. By becoming aware of our biases, seeking out new perspectives, actively listening to others, and engaging in self-reflection, we can develop a more accurate and truthful view of the world around us. This, in turn, can lead to more honest and authentic interactions with others, and ultimately, to stronger and more meaningful relationships.

The Road to Self-Awareness: Understanding the Role of Reflection, Feedback, and Self-Evaluation in Personal and Professional Growth.

 Self-awareness is an essential component of personal and professional growth. It is the foundation upon which we build our values, beliefs, and actions. Self-awareness is the ability to recognize our emotions, behaviors, and thought patterns and understand how they affect us and those around us. By acknowledging our strengths and weaknesses, we can make conscious decisions that lead to personal and professional success.

Self-reflection is a powerful tool for developing self-awareness. It involves taking time to evaluate our thoughts, feelings, and actions to gain insight into our behavior. When we engage in self-reflection, we become more aware of our emotions, patterns of behavior, and areas for improvement.

Feedback is another crucial element in building self-awareness. Receiving feedback from others can help us gain a different perspective on our behavior, identifying areas we may not have been aware of. Although it can be challenging to receive feedback, it provides a unique opportunity for growth and development.

Self-evaluation is the process of assessing our performance and progress towards our goals. By setting realistic and measurable goals, we can evaluate our progress and identify areas where we need to improve. This process can help us stay focused and motivated towards achieving our goals.

Realistic human behavior often involves struggles with self-awareness. For instance, when we encounter criticism or negative feedback, it can be difficult to accept it and reflect on our behavior. Our natural tendency is to become defensive and avoid admitting our faults. However, it is essential to recognize that criticism can provide valuable insight and help us identify areas where we need to improve.

In the rhythm of life, personal and professional growth requires constant self-evaluation, reflection, and feedback. By taking the time to examine our behavior, we can identify limiting beliefs, biases, and assumptions that may be holding us back. By challenging these beliefs and assumptions, we can cultivate a culture of honesty, self-awareness, and personal growth. Ultimately, developing self-awareness is not a one-time event, but a continuous process that requires consistent effort and an open mind.

COMMUNICATING WITH HONESTY

COMMUNICATING WITH HONESTY

Effective communication is the foundation of every relationship, personal or professional. However, communication becomes truly effective only when it is honest and truthful. Being honest in communication is not always easy, as it requires a great deal of vulnerability and transparency. It is essential to communicate with honesty to build trust, respect, and understanding.

Human behavior is complex, and often, our actions and words are influenced by a variety of factors, including our emotions, beliefs, and past experiences. When we communicate, we are not just transmitting information, but also sending signals about our thoughts, intentions, and emotions. Realistic human behavior plays a critical role in effective communication, as it allows us to understand the motives and needs of the people we are interacting with.

In today's fast-paced world, communication has become more critical than ever. With the advent of social media and other digital platforms, people are communicating more frequently and at a faster pace than ever before. However, with this increase in communication, there has also been a rise in miscommunication, misunderstanding, and dishonesty.

To communicate effectively, it is essential to be honest and transparent in our interactions. This involves not just saying what we mean but also listening and understanding the perspectives of others. Honest communication requires courage and vulnerability, as it often involves expressing our true feelings, even when they are difficult to articulate.

In this age of information, communicating with honesty is more critical than ever. It allows us to build trust, create meaningful relationships, and navigate complex social situations. By being honest in our communication, we can improve our personal and professional lives, and create a more connected and authentic world.

Strategies for being honest in difficult conversations

Difficult conversations can be some of the most challenging moments in life. It takes a lot of courage to be honest and vulnerable during these types of conversations. However, avoiding these conversations can lead to resentment and frustration, which can damage relationships. Therefore, it is important to have strategies in place for being honest during difficult conversations.

The first step is to approach the conversation with the right mindset. It's important to remember that the goal of the conversation is to find a solution or reach an understanding, not to prove yourself right or to make the other person feel bad. It's important to approach the conversation with a sense of empathy and understanding for the other person's perspective.

The second strategy is active listening. Active listening is an essential tool for promoting truthfulness in communication. It involves listening with an open mind and without judgment, paying close attention to the speaker's words, body language, and tone of voice. It's important to ask clarifying questions and paraphrase what you heard to ensure that you understand the other person's perspective correctly.

The third strategy is to be honest and clear in your communication. It's important to express your thoughts and feelings in a way that is respectful and non-confrontational. Use "I" statements instead of "you" statements to avoid blaming the other person. For example, instead of saying, "You always make me feel frustrated," say, "I feel frustrated when this happens."

The fourth strategy is to stay calm and avoid getting defensive. It's natural to feel defensive during difficult conversations, but it's important to remain calm and avoid reacting impulsively. Take a deep breath, and remind yourself of the goal of the conversation. If you feel yourself getting too emotional, it's okay to take a break and come back to the conversation later.

The fifth and final strategy is to be open to feedback. It's important to remember that difficult conversations are an opportunity for growth and learning. Be open to feedback from the other person, and be willing to make changes if necessary. It takes courage and vulnerability to be honest during difficult conversations, but the rewards are worth it. By using these strategies, you can promote truthfulness in communication and build stronger, more honest relationships.

"The Power of Vulnerability: How Authenticity Leads to Better Communication"

In our society, vulnerability is often seen as a weakness. People may think that showing vulnerability makes them look weak or that it leaves them open to being hurt or taken advantage of. However, vulnerability is actually a strength, and it can lead to better communication and more authentic connections between people.

Being vulnerable means being open and honest about your thoughts, feelings, and experiences. It means being willing to share your true self with others and to be seen as you really are. This can be scary, especially if you have been hurt in the past, but it is an important part of building trust and intimacy in relationships.

One way that vulnerability leads to better communication is that it allows for more open and honest conversations. When we are willing to share our thoughts and feelings, even if they are difficult or uncomfortable, we create a space for others to do the same. This can lead to deeper understanding and a greater sense of empathy between people.

Vulnerability also allows us to connect with others on a deeper level. When we are open and honest about who we are, we allow others to see us for who we really are, and this can create a strong sense of connection and trust. It can also lead to a greater sense of compassion and understanding for others, as we realize that we all have struggles and challenges in our lives.

It's important to remember that vulnerability is not the same as weakness. In fact, it takes a great deal of strength and courage to be vulnerable, especially in a society that often values toughness and stoicism. When we are vulnerable, we are showing others that we trust them and that we are willing to be open and honest with them.

However, it's also important to be mindful of the people with whom we choose to be vulnerable. Not everyone is deserving of our trust, and it's important to be discerning about who we share our innermost thoughts and feelings with. We should also be careful not to overshare or to use vulnerability as a way to manipulate others or gain sympathy.

the power of vulnerability should not be underestimated. It can lead to more honest and authentic communication, stronger connections and trust, and a greater sense of compassion and understanding for others. While it can be scary to be vulnerable, it is an important part of personal growth and can lead to a more fulfilling and meaningful life.

"From Conflict to Connection: Strategies for Navigating Tough Conversations"

From personal relationships to professional settings, tough conversations are an inevitable part of life. Whether it's addressing issues with a partner, having a difficult conversation with a colleague or delivering constructive feedback to an employee, these conversations can be stressful and challenging. However, avoiding them can lead to further problems, and not addressing them can hinder personal and professional growth.

One of the keys to successfully navigating tough conversations is through effective communication. Active listening is an important component of communication, and it involves being present and attentive during the conversation. It requires setting aside distractions, maintaining eye contact, and showing empathy to the speaker. By being an active listener, one can better understand the other person's point of view, which can lead to a more productive and positive conversation.

Another important aspect of successful communication is clear and direct communication. This involves using simple and straightforward language, and avoiding ambiguity or indirectness. Being clear and direct can help prevent misunderstandings and confusion, which can further complicate the conversation.

In addition to effective communication, it is important to approach tough conversations with an open and non-judgmental mindset. This involves setting aside preconceived notions and biases, and being open to the other person's perspective. It is also important to approach the conversation with a sense of curiosity and willingness to learn, which can help promote a more productive and respectful conversation.

Another key strategy for navigating tough conversations is to address the problem or issue directly and to avoid attacking the person. This involves focusing on the behavior or action rather than the person themselves. By doing this, it helps the other person feel heard and understood, which can lead to a more collaborative and respectful conversation.

Furthermore, it is essential to be honest and transparent during tough conversations. This involves being honest about one's own feelings and perspectives, and also being willing to listen to and consider the other person's feelings and perspectives. Being honest and transparent can promote trust and understanding, which can lead to more successful conversations.

Lastly, it is important to maintain a level of professionalism and respect during tough conversations. This involves avoiding personal attacks or insults, and being mindful of one's tone and body language. Maintaining professionalism and respect can help promote a more productive and positive conversation, even in challenging situations.

tough conversations are an unavoidable aspect of life. By using effective communication, approaching the conversation with an open and non-judgmental mindset, addressing the problem directly, being honest and transparent, and maintaining professionalism and respect, one can navigate these conversations more successfully. With practice and perseverance, these strategies can become second nature, leading to improved personal and professional relationships.

"Breaking the Cycle of Dishonesty: Overcoming the Fear of Being Honest in Tough Conversations"

Honest communication can be challenging, especially when it comes to discussing difficult or sensitive topics. People often avoid these conversations out of fear of hurting others, making themselves vulnerable, or damaging relationships. However, avoiding these conversations can lead to greater problems and hinder the growth of personal and professional relationships. Breaking the cycle of dishonesty involves overcoming the fear of being honest in tough conversations.

One strategy for overcoming this fear is to start by acknowledging and accepting the discomfort that comes with having difficult conversations. It is natural to feel anxious or fearful about speaking your mind, but it is important to remember that avoiding these conversations can have more significant negative consequences in the long run. By recognizing that discomfort is a normal part of honest communication, you can begin to face the fear head-on and start to take steps towards having more productive conversations.

Another helpful strategy is to focus on the intended outcome of the conversation. While it may be tempting to simply vent or criticize, the ultimate goal of the conversation should be to improve the situation and strengthen the relationship. This means approaching the conversation with a mindset of empathy and respect, and keeping an open mind to different perspectives. When both parties can feel heard and understood, they are more likely to work together to find a solution that benefits everyone.

It is also essential to be clear and direct in communication, and to avoid passive-aggressive behavior or avoidance tactics. Being honest about your thoughts and feelings can be uncomfortable, but it can also be liberating and lead to greater trust and respect in the relationship. When there is a lack of clarity or honesty, misunderstandings and misinterpretations can occur, leading to further conflict or resentment.

Finally, it is important to practice active listening in tough conversations. This involves truly listening to the other person's perspective and feelings without interrupting or dismissing them. Active listening can help to build empathy, trust, and understanding between both parties. When people feel heard and understood, they are more likely to reciprocate and listen openly to your perspective as well.

overcoming the fear of being honest in tough conversations is essential for breaking the cycle of dishonesty and promoting more authentic communication. By acknowledging discomfort, focusing on the intended outcome, being direct and clear, and practicing active listening, individuals can approach difficult conversations with greater confidence and success.

The role of active listening in promoting truthfulness in communication

Effective communication is crucial in every relationship, personal or professional. A crucial component of effective communication is active listening, which can play a significant role in promoting truthfulness in communication. Active listening is the ability to fully concentrate on and understand what the other person is saying, and then respond appropriately. When we practice active listening, we demonstrate that we value the speaker's opinion and are open to hearing what they have to say. This approach to communication creates a safe space for honesty and transparency.

One way that active listening promotes truthfulness in communication is by creating a supportive environment that encourages the speaker to be honest. People are more likely to share their thoughts and feelings when they feel that they are being heard and understood. Active listening ensures that the speaker feels seen, heard, and valued. As a result, they are more likely to be forthcoming and truthful in their communication.

Another way that active listening promotes truthfulness in communication is by allowing the listener to gain a better understanding of the speaker's perspective. When we actively listen, we make an effort to understand the speaker's point of view, even if we don't agree with it. This understanding can lead to a deeper level of empathy and appreciation for the speaker's perspective, which can ultimately lead to better communication and a more honest and transparent conversation.

In addition, active listening can help identify potential areas of disagreement, allowing the listener to address potential concerns or misunderstandings before they become larger problems. By actively listening, we can ask clarifying questions, confirm our understanding of the speaker's thoughts and feelings, and address any concerns or misunderstandings that we may have. This proactive approach to communication helps to foster honesty and transparency by identifying and addressing potential conflicts early on.

Overall, active listening is a vital skill in promoting truthfulness in communication. By creating a supportive environment, promoting understanding and empathy, and addressing potential concerns or misunderstandings, active listening helps to build a foundation of trust and honesty in any relationship. When we actively listen to others, we demonstrate that we value their opinions and are open to hearing what they have to say. By doing so, we create an environment that encourages honesty and transparency, which ultimately leads to stronger and more meaningful relationships.

"The Art of Listening: How Active Listening Can Build Trust and Encourage Truthfulness in Communication"

Communication is an essential aspect of human interaction, and active listening plays a critical role in promoting truthfulness in communication. Active listening is the act of fully concentrating on what the speaker is saying, interpreting their message accurately, and responding appropriately. The art of listening involves not only hearing but also understanding and empathizing with the speaker's perspective.

Active listening begins with focusing on the speaker and creating an environment that encourages open and honest communication. It's important to set aside any distractions, make eye contact, and avoid interrupting the speaker. By providing this space for the speaker, they feel heard and respected, which is essential in building trust and encouraging truthfulness.

In addition to providing a safe space, active listening also involves actively engaging with the speaker. This means asking questions, seeking clarification, and reflecting back on what they said. By doing so, you're showing that you're invested in the conversation and committed to understanding their perspective. This fosters open and honest communication because the speaker feels heard and understood.

Another important aspect of active listening is acknowledging the speaker's feelings. Emotions are an essential part of human communication, and acknowledging them can help to build trust and encourage truthfulness. When you acknowledge someone's emotions, you're showing that you're aware of their perspective and are open to understanding their experience. This encourages them to be more honest and open about their thoughts and feelings.

Overall, active listening is a powerful tool in promoting truthfulness in communication. It requires creating a safe space, actively engaging with the speaker, and acknowledging their emotions. By doing so, you're showing that you're committed to understanding their perspective, which encourages open and honest communication.

"Breaking Down Barriers: The Role of Active Listening in Overcoming Communication Challenges and Fostering Honest Dialogue"

Effective communication is a cornerstone of any healthy relationship, be it personal or professional. Yet, despite the best of intentions, we all encounter communication challenges from time to time. These can arise from a variety of sources, such as differences in communication styles, preconceived biases, or simply a lack of active listening. In such situations, the role of active listening cannot be overstated. Active listening is a form of empathetic and attentive listening that seeks to understand the speaker's message, feelings, and intentions, without interruption or judgement.

Active listening begins with creating an environment that is conducive to open and honest communication. This can involve removing distractions, such as turning off electronic devices or finding a quiet space where both parties can feel comfortable. It also involves maintaining eye contact, using non-verbal cues, and focusing on the speaker's tone of voice and body language, as much as their words. Through active listening, we demonstrate to the speaker that we are invested in what they have to say and that their message matters.

However, active listening is not just about being present in the moment and hearing what the speaker has to say. It also involves asking clarifying questions, paraphrasing, and summarizing the speaker's message to ensure that we understand them correctly. This helps to avoid misunderstandings and allows the speaker to feel heard and validated. It also helps to build trust and to create an environment where honest communication can take place.

In the workplace, active listening is especially important when navigating complex or emotionally charged conversations. For example, when giving feedback or addressing performance issues with an employee, active listening can help to create an environment that is more conducive to learning and growth. By actively listening to the employee's perspective and concerns, we can build trust and understanding, and work collaboratively to identify solutions that benefit everyone.

Active listening can also be beneficial in personal relationships, such as with romantic partners, friends, or family members. When someone comes to us with a problem, listening actively and without judgment can help them to feel heard and understood, which can lead to more productive and effective problem-solving. It can also help to foster deeper connections and a stronger sense of mutual respect and empathy.

active listening is a crucial tool for promoting truthfulness in communication. By creating an environment of open and honest dialogue, and actively listening to what the speaker has to say, we can break down barriers to communication and build stronger relationships, both personal and professional.

Dear Readers

Dear Reader,

We wanted to take a moment to express our sincerest gratitude for taking the time to read our book, "Adopting the Total Mentality of Truthfulness." We understand that your time is precious, and we are humbled and honored that you chose to spend it with us.

We truly hope that the insights and strategies presented in this book have been helpful to you in your personal and professional growth. Our goal was to provide practical tools to help you cultivate a mindset of truthfulness, and we hope that you have found these strategies to be valuable in your life.

Please know that we are here for you on your journey towards living a life of honesty and authenticity. We would love to stay connected with you and continue to offer guidance and support. If you have any questions or would like to share your experience with us, please do not hesitate to reach out.

Thank you again for your support and for being a part of our community. We wish you all the best as you continue to adopt the total mentality of truthfulness.

Sincerely,

Anubhavauthor . . .

Notes

WRITER'S NOTE

Dear reader,

Are you tired of feeling like something is missing in your life? Do you long for deeper connections with those around you, or for a sense of purpose and meaning in your work? If so, then my book, "Adopting the Total Mentality of Truthfulness," is for you.

In this book, I delve into the power of truthfulness and how it can transform our personal and professional lives. Through my own experiences, as well as the insights of my mentors, I explore the ways in which honesty, integrity, and self-reflection can help us to create a more meaningful and fulfilling life.

I believe that this book has the power to change your life. It is not just a collection of ideas or theories, but a practical guide to embracing a total mentality of truthfulness. Whether you are struggling in your relationships, feeling unfulfilled in your career, or simply seeking a greater sense of purpose and meaning, this book offers practical strategies for achieving lasting change.

So if you are ready to take the first step towards a more authentic and fulfilling life, I encourage you to read "Adopting the Total Mentality of Truthfulness." I truly believe that it has the power to change your life in ways you never thought possible.

Buy: Original Copy at The Publisher of Anubhav Shrivastava

This is not original book :-